GONE WEST!

Lee Madden's job is to protect a wagon train on its journey from Missouri to Oregon. But his past catches up with him in the brutal shape of Deacon Swain, a border ruffian out to avenge the killing of his younger brother. There are compensations, though. After a vicious clash with Pawnee Indians, Lee finds himself increasingly attracted to the newly widowed Martha. Can their relationship survive both his deadly feud with Swain and a determined assault on the wagon train by Sioux Indians in the foothills of the Rockies?

PAUL BEDFORD

◆

GONE WEST!

Complete and Unabridged

LINFORD
Leicester

First published in Great Britain in 2016 by
Robert Hale
an imprint of The Crowood Press
Wiltshire

First Linford Edition
published 2020
by arrangement with
The Crowood Press
Wiltshire

A catalogue record for this book is available
from the British Library.

ISBN 978–1–4448–4367–5

Published by
F. A. Thorpe (Publishing)
Anstey, Leicestershire

Set by Words & Graphics Ltd.
Anstey, Leicestershire
Printed and bound in Great Britain by
T. J. International Ltd., Padstow, Cornwall

This book is printed on acid-free paper

1

Jake Twelvetrees wasn't used to being pressed on his decisions and it didn't sit well. 'You want me, you got him too,' he barked.

Ten pairs of resentful eyes switched from him to the subject of their ire and then back again. One man, bolder than the rest, wasn't prepared to leave it there. 'Well I say he's got no right coming along. Every one of us has paid good cash money to join this wagon train, but we ain't seen a dime of his yet,' complained Rufus Barlow. 'And why did he wait 'til Nebraska? Everyone knows Independence, Missouri's the starting point?'

'What the hell does that matter?' Jake protested. 'He's here now, isn't he?'

'Yeah, but is he?' responded the other man quizzically. 'We're supposed to be heading west aren't we? Yet he spends most of his time gazing south to Kansas? What's that all about, huh?'

There were grunts of agreement from his companions, causing Jake to sigh impatiently. He was a bluff, broad shouldered ex-soldier who had been hired to get a job done. 'I haven't got time for all this. We're burning daylight and Bent's going to think we've bust an axle or run into the Pawnee or some such.' Gesturing over towards Lee Madden's unhelpfully silent figure, he said firmly, 'I've known this man for more years than I care to think on. He's got hidden talents that you folks might just be glad of on the journey ahead. So I'll say this one more time. Unless you want me to head on back to Independence to lead another train, he stays!'

Some of the cooler heads amongst the group had the sense to realize that if he wasn't bluffing, then they would effectively find themselves without a leader and that thought didn't appeal. 'C'mon Rufus,' muttered one of them. 'No good will come of this and who knows, this fella might just turn out to be a 'snake oil' salesman. Then you could buy a bottle of elixir and lubricate that sour tongue of yours.'

That drew a few laughs and the tension seemed to drain out of the atmosphere. Barlow huffed and puffed, but he knew he'd lost his audience. He turned back towards his wagon, but not before casting a dark glance in Madden's direction.

Finally left alone with his friend, Jake gave vent to a little frustration. 'Great help you turned out to be. You might at least have said something in your defence!'

Lee Madden favoured him with a strangely sad smile. 'You seemed to be doing all right without me. Besides, they're right. I haven't put up any money.'

Jake returned the smile, although with considerably more vigour. 'And so long as I'm captain of this train, you won't have to. Since the forty-niners and all the other riff-raff that headed for California stirred up the Indians, settlers have to travel in large parties for protection. I've got forty prairie schooners to look after, so I'm surely entitled to a deputy. I'm mighty glad that you happened upon us, although I've got to admit I'm curious as to just what brings you out here.'

A cloud seemed to fall over Lee Madden's broad face. 'Let's just leave that for another time. I'm grateful for your support, Jake. I really am. But I ain't in the mood to answer questions right now and in any case these folks seem anxious to be on the move.' With that, he heaved his solid frame up into his saddle and motioned his horse well out on to the south flank of the westward-headed wagon train. He had no intention of eating other people's dust for the 2,000 miles that he'd heard they would need to travel to reach Oregon Territory.

As he gazed along the line of creaking wagons making their way across the seemingly endless plains, Lee wondered just how many of the hopeful pioneers would actually reach that far-off destination. Hell, on a clear night, even the moon seemed nearer than the west coast. To attempt such a journey with young children and even a few elderly relatives seemed hopelessly optimistic, especially now that many of the wild tribes were known to be hostile to the overlanders. But then violence was something that Lee knew plenty about and the colour of a man's skin really didn't alter the nature of conflict.

As the miles passed, his body settled into the rhythm of his animal's steady walk and his mind began that unavoidable drift back into the recent past. The bleak memories seemed to haunt his every waking moment, but maybe . . . just maybe with the passing of time and distance they might begin to dim. The question permanently gnawing at him was would he be left in peace to start his new life?

★　★　★

5

In that year of 1857, the residents of Topeka were sadly used to outbreaks of violence in their community. As 'free soilers', bitterly opposed to the spread of slavery, they were constantly on the watch for marauding gangs of pro-slavery supporters. The widespread festering conflict had led to the territory being dubbed 'Bleeding Kansas' by New York Tribune editor Horace Greeley. Located on a ferry crossing traversing the Kansas River, the town also received frequent, but far more peaceful visits from passing wagon trains heading west. It was through here that Jake Twelvetrees and his party had passed some two weeks earlier.

The gang of 'border ruffians' that reined in amongst a grove of trees located just beyond the outermost buildings was different from the usual bands of trouble causers. The seven men arrived in the dead of night and weren't interested in random violence and property damage. All their thoughts were focused on one particular house. After handing the reins to the youngest of the group, six of them padded silently towards the darkened streets. Like many of their ilk, they favoured fearsome broadswords for intimidation and carried 'cap and ball' revolvers for self-defence.

Their leader believed that he knew exactly where he was going. He was a large unkempt brute with an excessive fondness for corn whiskey. His name was Deacon Swain and behind his wild eyes there lurked a dangerously unbalanced intellect. As a native of South Carolina, he felt himself to be in enemy territory, but there was an unusually pressing reason for his presence in Topeka.

They were in amongst the simple timber buildings when Swain suddenly motioned the others to a halt. As his companions nervously fingered their weapons, he peered around at the darkened houses in an attempt to get his bearings. He had only been to the town once before and that had been in daylight. Damn, but things looked so different at night!

As his eyes desperately swivelled about, they alighted on a window in the nearest property and his heart abruptly jumped with shock. There, staring back in abject terror was the ghostly face of a young girl. As though swaying on trembling feet, her nose suddenly pressed up against a pane of distorted, poorly manufactured glass. Probably just using the piss pot, he surmised, but there was no denying she had given him a jolt. And the question was, would she scream?

Swain slowly raised his right forefinger to his lips and nodded encouragingly. The girl's eyes widened like saucers and then her face abruptly disappeared. He stood like a statue for what seemed an age, but mercifully the silence remained unbroken. Quite probably she had padded back to bed, to recollect the strange sighting as a bad dream the next morning.

Lucky for her, he decided. If they had been hindered in their purpose, he would doubtless have slaughtered the child and all her family and felt justified in doing so . . . until remorse set in later, as had happened so often in his life. Leading the others away, he heaved a great sigh of relief and then by immense good fortune suddenly saw exactly what he was looking for. An off-white picket fence showed up dully against the darker single storey structure behind it.

'Remember,' hissed Swain. 'No noise and no killing until I say so. It's answers I need, first.'

With exaggerated care, he opened the gate and led his five thugs over to the front door of the simple dwelling. As expected in such lawless times it was locked, but they had come prepared. A crowbar split the poorly seasoned wood and then they were crowding into the parlour.

At least one of the occupants was a light sleeper and a male voice cried out from the back room, 'Who is it? What do you want?'

Swain gestured for his men to surround the door and when it was flung open they rushed into the room with drawn swords. There was a brief struggle, followed by a female's high-pitched scream that was immediately curtailed. As their leader watched, the men dragged a solidly built individual out of the bedroom.

'Who all else is in there?' Swain demanded.

'Just the lady of the house,' replied one of his men with a snigger. 'She's chewing on my kerchief at the minute.'

Now the thought of that tickled Deacon Swain. 'Then God help her,' he guffawed. 'That verminous rag hasn't seen a wash tub in many a long year. Just you keep her in there, while I find out how helpful her man is going to be.' He switched his attention to one of the others. 'Joe, get that lamp to working. I want to take a better look at this son of a bitch.'

As that man did as instructed, the others forced their prisoner down into a solid-looking rocking chair. As a lucifer flared up, followed by the lamp itself, the sudden illumination caused all of them to blink. As their captive gazed around at the menacing intruders, his shocked expression changed to one of real fear.

'Take anything you want,' he blurted out. 'Just don't harm my wife!'

Swain took a good long look at him before responding. He noted the solid, chunky physique and the strong jaw under a luxuriant moustache. He decided that they might well have to beat on him for an awful long time, in order to extract any useful information. Conveniently, there happened to be an alternative.

'It's funny you should say that,' he finally responded. 'Because if you don't tell me what I want to know, that's exactly what we'll do. And there's various ways to do hurt to a female. Savvy?'

Liam Madden gazed up at his tormentor in horrified silence, before again taking in the border ruffians and their vicious-looking broadswords. Then a look of resignation spread across his features as he posed the question that, in truth, he already knew the answer to. 'What do you want?'

Swain favoured him with a broad smile that completely failed to reach his eyes. 'You don't look like a halfwit to me, so I reckon this won't come as a surprise. Where's your brother?'

Liam's heart sank, but he made a mighty good job of concealing it. 'I haven't seen Lee in years. There's a lot of things we don't agree on.'

The other man's smile slipped and he shook his head sadly. 'And there was me thinking we could avoid any carnage.' He jerked his head towards the bedroom door. 'Brady, pull that rag out of the bitch's mouth and saw a finger off. Nice and slow like.'

'Which one, boss?' came the improbable response.

Swain shook his head in apparent despair. 'I don't care, you moron. Pick one. Any one. It's your treat.'

In the bedroom, Brady tingled with anticipation. He was a buck-toothed rancid individual, who took pleasure in dispensing pain to others. Clambering on to the bed, he straddled the terrified woman and abruptly yanked the foul kerchief from her mouth. As he seized her right hand, she emitted a piercing scream, which of course was exactly the reaction that Swain had anticipated.

'He's gone west,' yelled Liam in desperation.

'Where west?' demanded his persecutor stridently.

'Oregon. Well away from this madness. He's had enough of it all.'

'Well we haven't had enough of *him*. He killed my kid brother and us Swains live by the feud.' Anger and bitterness coloured his words, but then he exhibited one of his lightning mercurial mood swings and nodded with apparent satisfaction. Backing off, Deacon

Swain theatrically sauntered into the bedroom. 'Thank you, ma'am,' he announced with mock civility. 'We've got what we came for, so we'll be taking our leave.' Strangely, he then snatched one of the pillows, which only added to the woman's alarm.

'How's about I slice her up anyway?' asked Brady hopefully.

Swain glanced at him bleakly. 'I reckon not. Butchering some female ain't going to help our cause any. But, we do need to make an example.' So saying, he swept back into the parlour, placed the pillow over Liam's face and pulled out his Colt Navy. 'Hold him tight, boys.'

'Why don't you use your sword?' asked Joe hopefully.

There was an ominous metallic double-click, as the hammer was retracted on the revolver. ''Cause I don't want to be wiping pieces of him off me for the rest of the night. That's why,' replied Swain sharply and then he squeezed the trigger.

2

The gunshot, one amongst an inter-mittent barrage, went completely unnoticed. It was the resulting high-pitched scream that suddenly cut through him like a razor. Jerked out of his reverie, Lee Madden urged his mount over towards the head of the wagon train. Fifty yards or so in front of the lead vehicle, a young man lay on the ground. His features were contorted in agony as he clutched his left thigh. By his side was a smoking revolver. It was immediately apparent what had happened. Yet another firearms accident!

As the travellers had advanced across the plains on the north bank of the Little Blue River, they had been amazed and frightened at the number of snakes that they had encountered. With their oxen plodding along in front of the wagons, numerous serpents slithered away from the animals' hooves. Against the advice of their guide, the wagoners relentlessly killed the creatures with their guns and whips, as though seeking to exterminate the whole species. The crackle of musketry had become an almost ever-present feature of the journey, along with the relentless creak of wood and leather. Unfortunately, so many firearms in inexperienced hands had led to a rash of accidents.

As the boy's family rushed over, his mother wailed piteously, 'Sweet Jesus, Thad's like to die from this!'

As calmer heads viewed the injury, one man stated, 'It's just a flesh wound, is all. The ball's missed bone and gone straight through. It just needs binding up.'

Lee, mindful of his precarious position in the train, had kept his distance until his practised eye spotted something that could not be ignored. Dismounting, he shouldered his way through the throng. 'If that's all you do, it'll likely infect and he'll die,' he stated flatly.

'What the hell would you know about any of it?' barked out Rufus Barlow belligerently. That man obviously still hadn't accepted Lee's continued presence amongst them.

The newcomer eyed him coldly. He was minded to turn away and leave them to it, but in all conscience he couldn't just leave young Thad to a ghastly death.

'Mister, if you had half a brain, you'd know that with this kind of injury it's not the ball that's dangerous, but whatever might have been carried into the body with it. Believe me, I've seen more than enough gunshot wounds.'

Barlow bristled with anger at the other man's scathing attitude and therefore missed the apparent reference to Lee's violent past. 'Just what are you saying, Madden?'

'What I'm saying, is that if you look closely you'll see there's a piece of his pants leg missing. I'd lay odds that it's still in the wound and needs fetching out, pronto!'

The boy's father was on the point of cutting the material away and he momentarily froze with the shock of recognition. 'By God, this fella's right.' Turning to his nearest neighbour, he instructed, 'Here, help me lift Thad to our wagon. And somebody light a fire. We're going to need hot water when we probe his leg.'

With blood flowing from the wound and the boy's mother fussing around, there were plenty of willing hands to help out. As Lee backed off to leave them to it, he called out, 'And some whiskey wouldn't hurt. On the wound and down the throat.' Snatching a glance at the sour-faced Rufus Barlow, he flippantly added, 'And tell any Temperance Movement that happens by that it's purely medicinal!'

He looked up as Jake Twelvetrees arrived from the rear of the long column. 'So another would-be hunter's blown a hole in himself,' that man observed sadly. 'I keep telling them to leave the goddamned snakes alone. There's more folk getting shot than bit.' The wagon train leader glanced down at Thad's discarded Colt Dragoon. Shaking his head, he remarked, 'And what the hell is a young lad doing with a horse pistol like that? His pa ought to know better. The recoil alone's enough to put him on his back!'

Lee chuckled at that, but before he had chance to comment, a cry went up from the rider on point duty. 'Bent's coming in at a trot, Jake. Looks like he's got something on his mind.'

'That man always has,' muttered Jake only half to himself as he dismounted. 'I'm sure he likes to put on a show to justify his fee, but there's no denying that he knows his business. And the lives of well over one hundred souls depend on that.'

William Bent had been ranging far and wide around the train for some days and so he and Lee had not yet met. As the mountain-man-turned-scout approached the wagon train, Lee took the opportunity to scrutinize him. He was given plenty of time because the other man stopped to have brief words with the individual on point. What he saw was pretty much as expected. The buckskin-clad frontiersman was lean and rangy, with eyes that seemed to permanently roam the horizon. He carried a once highly prized, large calibre muzzle-loaded Hawken rifle across his saddle horn, ready for instant use. Two rather more modern revolvers were also tucked into his belt, providing him with an enviable firepower. Because of Bent's wide-brimmed hat, it was only when he reined in before the two waiting men that his prematurely white flowing hair became clearly visible. Lee was musing on the probable cause of that when he suddenly became aware that the frontiersman had settled a pair of piercing eyes on him.

'You've certainly taken a good close

look at me, mister. I reckon it's time we was properly introduced.'

Jake chuckled appreciatively. 'This man just doesn't miss a trick. Will, this is Lee Madden, an old friend of mine. We served in the Mexican War together and kind of watched each other's backs. You know how it is.'

Bent was just on the point of responding to that when there was a penetrating scream in one of the wagons. Sliding a leg over the saddle horn, he lithely dropped to the ground. 'Don't tell me. Another one of these damn fool pilgrims has shot himself.'

Jake nodded regretfully. 'Ethan Wells' boy. They're working on him now. With luck he'll be hobbling around afore too long.'

'Yeah, yeah,' grunted Bent with an obvious lack of interest. It was plain that something of greater moment was preying on his mind. Leaning forward, he shook hands with Lee and then got straight to the point. 'If we ain't mighty careful, there's likely to be a lot more

21

bloodletting around these parts soon.'

Jake's response was instantaneous. 'That can only mean you've spotted some hostiles.'

The scout nodded grimly. 'Ain't met a Pawnee yet who wasn't. I came across a war party of them, just south of the Platte River. About forty of the devils, I reckon and they're heading this way. Since we've got to follow the Platte west, there's really no way to avoid them.'

Every single wagon train had one golden rule; follow the rivers. To ignore that meant courting certain death.

Lee had just the one question. 'I've never encountered any Pawnee. What can we expect from them?'

Bent deliberated briefly before giving his considered opinion. 'Their natural enemies are the Sioux, but once they trip over us, they'll want anything they can get. I reckon we're too big a party for them to launch an all-out assault on, so they'll call a parley and then expect gifts. Lots of gifts! If they don't get them, they'll be a thorn in our side for days to come.'

Jake Twelvetrees spat a gobbet of phlegm on to the grass. 'I don't favour giving presents to the wild tribes. If they continue getting something for nothing, they'll just keep coming back.'

The white-haired scout shrugged non-committedly. 'They don't see it that way. In their eyes we're just paying tribute to cross their land.'

Jake had heard enough. 'This land belongs to the United States of America. If they can't accept that, then the only tribute they'll get from us is with powder and lead!'

Lee gestured off to the west. 'Looks like you might have to put that to the test. That point man sure is in a hurry.'

The rider spurred his animal to the head of the column and frantically pointed off into the distance, but by then his news was already old news. Spread along the westward horizon was a clearly visible line of slowly advancing horsemen. Although their immediate intentions were unclear, there was no doubt at all that they weren't just passing through. It was time for Jake Twelvetrees to earn his pay and make some command decisions. Thankfully he was up to the task. Scrambling into the saddle, he called to Lee, 'Follow me,' and then spurred over to the lead wagon.

The convoy had not yet restarted following the shooting incident, so it was easy for Jake to make himself understood. As was often the case, the family of four had been walking along next to their wagon rather than riding aboard it, so as to spare the oxen and consequently were huddled together on the grass. From the expressions on their faces it was obvious that the two adults recognized the imminent danger.

'We've likely got Indian trouble, Chandler,' announced Jake gravely. 'I want you to wheel your wagon around in a complete circle, large enough to take all the others and then arm yourself and join me and Bent. Wife and children under the wagon, with firearms if they've got them.' Then, turning to his companion he continued, 'Lee, I'd take it real kindly if you'd ride past each wagon and tell them to follow on and do the same thing. After that I want every man out front here with his long gun for a show of force. Tell Ethan Wells he's excused if he's still seeing to Thad.' With that, he steered his horse around and rejoined William Bent.

As Lee made his way down the long column, he relayed Jake's instructions to each and every family, including an apparently permanently sour Rufus Barlow. 'Why didn't we take another route and avoid those godless hea-thens?' that man queried.

Lee attempted to maintain a reason-able demeanour. 'Well I ain't no mountain man, Mr Barlow, but I do know that if any of us are to survive this journey then we've got to stay with the rivers.' But then he just couldn't resist a little dig. 'Oh, and I'm not a believer either, but don't fret. I'm not after your scalp. Yet!'

Barlow's wife glared at the messenger. 'I don't think I like your tone, Mr Madden!'

'Well I'll tell you ma'am, you're not the first to say it, but then some people are just all shit and no sugar.' Leaving her to digest that ambiguous remark, he touched his hat and moved swiftly on to the next wagon. He knew that he hadn't done himself any favours, but then in truth he no longer really cared what people thought of him.

It just so happened that Ethan Wells regarded the approaching rider with a sight more esteem. 'I'm obliged to you for your advice, mister. I reckon you might well have saved Thad's life or at the very least, his leg.'

Lee favoured him with a genuine smile. 'Well I'm right glad to hear that, but we may well be all fighting for our own soon, so I'd keep that horse pistol close.'

★ ★ ★

By the time the wagon train had formed a circle, the Pawnee war party had halted a mere 200 yards away. That was hopelessly out of range for any revolver, but a reasonable distance for a sharp eye with a long gun.

'What do you reckon then, Will?' Jake demanded. 'I'm no Indian fighter and those sure ain't Mexicans out there.'

The mountain man viewed the opposing force with surprising calm. 'As I said before, they're most likely expecting tribute. It would behove us to have a parley, although you haven't left me much to bargain with.' Briefly he glanced back at the white men milling around nervously in front of the wagons and grunted scornfully. 'You'd better stay here and look after your 'army'. Make sure no one pops a cap by mistake or we'll end up with more than any mere shooting accident.' Switching his attention to Lee, he added, 'I'll take your deputy along for support.'

As the two men slowly moved off, Jake called out, 'Remember, those sons of bitches get nothing from us!'

Bent made no acknowledgement. Instead he murmured to Lee, 'Your friend is making a big mistake.'

The other man expected him to elaborate, but nothing more was forthcoming and so together they approached the waiting Indians. As they drew closer and saw exactly what they were up against, Lee had to make a conscious effort not to reach for a weapon. To a supposedly 'civilized' white man, the warriors presented a terrifyingly primitive sight. All of them were garishly daubed in paint and had removed most of their hair, so that only a tufted patch remained along the top of their skulls. Into this had been tied feathers of varying sizes and hues.

Each member of the war party was armed to the teeth with bows and arrows, lances, axes and knives of various sizes. Very few carried firearms and then only 'trade' muskets, probably as a mark of status. In the late spring warmth, most of them wore only a breechclout, but then Lee spotted something that made his blood run cold. One of the Indians had a blue US Army greatcoat draped over his shoulders. A long dried, dark stain was clearly visible on the left breast, providing incontrovertible proof that the Indians were most definitely hostile.

Lee inhaled a deep breath in an attempt to steady his nerves. From beside him Bent hissed, 'Don't scare! If they sense fear, we're both finished.'

Easier said than done, Lee decided, but then an idea occurred to him. He would focus all his attention on one person and wait on events. As the two men came to a halt about twenty feet away from the menacing horde, he resolutely fixed his eyes on those of the greatcoat's owner. That individual possessed a malevolent expression that hinted at a great hatred of the white race in general. Recognizing an implied challenge, he fingered his lance and glared ferociously at the intruder.

With a baffling mixture of grunts and gestures, William Bent suddenly opened a dialogue with the Pawnee. He kept this up for some time, before their leader abruptly interrupted with what appeared to be a series of accusations and demands. Finally motioning towards the wagons, that man displayed the fingers and thumbs of both hands and then closed them in a grabbing movement. Even Lee was left in no doubt as to his meaning. The chief had demanded ten of their animals in exchange for the wagon train's safe passage.

Out of his peripheral vision, Lee was aware of Bent emphatically shaking his head before snapping out an instruction. 'Slowly place your hand on that Colt, but don't draw it. Try to look mean. Plenty mean!'

Throughout his adult life, Lee Madden had been involved in numerous violent encounters and he drew on that experience now. Visibly gritting his teeth, he gradually eased his right hand on to his Navy revolver. As his fingers closed over the smooth butt, he theatrically ran slitted eyes over the serried ranks before him. The response was quite literally hair-raising. In an almost feral display of anger, the braves whooped and howled and Lee was convinced that they were going to rush him. Somehow he just managed to control his horse and with Bent keeping station at his side, together they faced down the enraged Pawnees.

After several unbearably tense minutes of this, the Indians suddenly became distracted by some activity behind the two white men. Bent took that as his cue to retreat and called over to Lee, 'Start to back off, but don't take your eyes off these devils.' So saying, he urged his animal into an awkward reverse walk.

Gradually the two men began to put some distance between themselves and the menacing warriors. Emboldened by this, they swung around and headed for the relative safety of the wagons. It was only then that they realized why the Pawnees had held back. Jake Twelve-trees had organized the settlers into two ranks and all were pointing their rifles at the warriors. Even though many of the muzzles were shaking, the overall effect was impressive.

With a sigh of relief, Lee remarked, 'That Jake thinks he's still in the army and I for one am damned glad of it!'

'Now you know why my hair went white,' responded the scout with evident emotion. 'I've had too many run-ins like that.'

Lee regarded him with genuine admiration. 'It was certainly one too many for me and what the hell did you say to those demons, anyhu?'

'I told them that you were feared throughout the land. That your fire stick shoots many times, which is true. That you never miss, which may or may not be true and that all your *compadres* over by the wagon were exactly the same, which definitely ain't true.'

Lee chuckled, as much with relief as anything else. 'I'd heard you old-time mountain men were full of tall tales.'

As they approached Jake and his makeshift militia, Bent was suddenly grim faced, all traces of humour gone from his weather-beaten features. 'Well think on this. If I was at an old time rendezvous, I'd bet twenty prime beaver pelts that we hadn't seen the last of those goddamned Pawnees!'

3

As was to be expected, a gnawing sense of unease had descended upon the Oregon bound wagon train as it continued west on the so-called 'Platte River Road'. It was heightened by the fact that following the unsatisfactory standoff, the Pawnee war party had completely disappeared. Not even the redoubtable William Bent could find any trace of them. Despite that unsettling knowledge, Jake Twelvetrees had flatly refused to maintain the static defensive circle beyond the next sunrise. If they were to cross the Rockies before the winter snows and then go on to the west coast, it was essential that they kept moving. So from then on, everybody's waking moments were dominated by the contemplation of just where the Indians might be and if and when they would strike. As the wagons' occupants plodded across the seemingly limitless plains, all eyes were on the horizon. Any thoughts of shooting at serpents had completely dissipated, as all thoughts were turned to far more dangerous creatures.

During the stomach-churning hours of darkness, when every shadow resembled a painted savage, a double guard was officially maintained. In reality very few of the adults could get any shut-eye and their nerves were further taxed by the regular howling of wolves lurking beyond the encampment. Bent's claim that the animals were actually frightened of humans failed to reassure many of them.

In spite of, or possibly because of, their fear, a steady and acceptable pace of fifteen miles was maintained for each of the next four days. This brought them to early June and close to the junction of the North and South Platte Rivers. A crossing of the South Platte would soon be necessary to allow the train to continue on to Fort Laramie. It was that always-risky operation that had Jake especially worried.

'However you look at it, we're mighty vulnerable whenever we ford a stretch of water,' he confided to Lee. 'For a certain amount of time we will be desperately weaker on one bank than the other and there's not a damn thing we can do about it.'

The other man pondered the problem for a moment. 'We could split the men equally on each side and let the women and children drive the wagons across under cover of their guns. Those were the tactics we used in Mexico, remember?'

'Yeah, only then we had hard-fighting, hard-cussing freighters under our command, *not* women and children,' Jake responded gloomily.

'They won't have the strength to manage the oxen if they get out of control.' He was reflectively silent for a few seconds before shrugging his heavy shoulders. 'But I suppose you're right. It's our best and only chance.'

It was late in the afternoon when that day's hunting party returned. Unlike previous occasions its members all wore satisfied expressions. The area suddenly teemed with game and William Bent and his three companions had bagged two elk and one antelope. Such additions of fresh meat were particularly welcome as they added variety to a monotonous diet and helped fill out the gradually dwindling stores of bacon, flour, coffee, biscuits, etc. that had been taken on in Missouri.

The experienced scout also had news. 'Early tomorrow morning will see us at a fair river crossing. I used it easily and can guarantee your safety. It would behove us to take it, because after that the South Platte curves away fast.'

Jake's normally self-assured features registered unmistakeable anxiety. 'And what of the Pawnee? Have you found any sign of them?'

Bent shook his head emphatically.

'But that don't mean they're not about and I'll tell you something else. We're in for a real frog-strangler tonight, so we'll need to keep our powder dry.'

Jake pondered how the hell Bent knew that as he peered up at the cloudless and tranquil sky.

* * *

The wagon master never did find out the source of that prophecy, but as the sun began to set, black clouds did indeed boil in and he realized that they were all in for trouble. A chill swept over him as he recognized what needed to be done. Peremptorily, he summoned both Bent and Lee Madden. As the three of them congregated at the head of the wagon train, he kept moving as he informed them of his decision.

'I don't know how you knew, Will, but you were right about the storm. So we need to make a run for the river and cross over tonight before it gets dark.

When this downpour hits, the South Platte could well turn into a raging torrent and we'll be stuck for days.'

'That's madness,' the grizzled scout immediately asserted. 'If we try to rush a crossing with darkness coming on, we'll lose some people for sure. Why not just batten down and wait for it to subside? Then rest up and get more hunting in. With a group this size, there can never be too much fresh meat.'

Lee nodded his agreement. 'I reckon Will's right. It sounds too dangerous to me.'

' 'I reckon Will's right',' mimicked Jake scornfully. 'What the hell do you know about it? How many wagon trains have you escorted over the Rockies, huh? Don't you understand that we can't afford to dawdle around, losing time? If snow catches us in the Rockies we're all finished!' He stopped to take a breath. Deep down he knew that he had overreacted, but it wasn't his way to compromise and so he announced firmly, 'I'm master of this train, so you'll both do as I say. That's an order!'

Lee felt his hackles begin to rise. He felt beholden to his old comrade for giving him a job, but he was nobody's whipping boy. 'Fair enough,' he answered tightly. 'But if you get it wrong, don't ever give me another.'

Jake stared at him with mild surprise, before wheeling his animal away towards the lead wagon.

'Was he an officer in that there Mexican War?' queried Bent.

Lee nodded.

'That figures. From what I've heard they're all assholes!'

'Happen you've got that right,' responded Lee quietly. 'That's how my enlisted men thought of me . . . until they got to know me better.' With that the former lieutenant winked and then rode off after the wagon master.

★   ★   ★

Driven on by their leader's sense of urgency and repeated cajoling, the forty

40

wagons dramatically increased their pace. Unable to keep up on foot, the women and children climbed aboard as their men folk whipped the tired oxen on to greater efforts. In the lead wagon, Joshua Chandler smiled reassuringly at his wife, Martha, and instructed his two children to tighten the rear pucker straps on the double-thickness and supposedly rainproof canvas cover. He had not yet experienced a significant storm on the plains, but Captain Twelvetrees' dire warning had sunk in.

Chandler's particular position at the front of the train had not come about by chance. Independence, Missouri was the main outfitting centre for those heading west and it was there that he had impressed the captain with his apparent maturity and steadiness. So much so, that when the train finally set off he found himself assigned to the 'pole position', which meant that for the entire journey he would not have to eat other people's dust. Determined not to lose such an enviable situation, he cajoled yet more speed out of his unfortunate beasts.

Regrettably for all the overlanders, their efforts went unrewarded. A mile short of the South Platte crossing point, with daylight almost non-existent, the heavens opened with an almighty crash. A veritable torrent of cold water plummeted on to the abruptly struggling wagon train. As the grass grew slippery, their progress immediately slackened.

'Keep them moving,' Jake bellowed impatiently. 'We're nearly there. Lee, get down the line and tell them to haul ass!'

With the rain coming down in biblical quantities it was difficult even to see the way. All the wagon owners could do was cautiously follow the family in front and pray for the best. Chandler, anxiously perched on the edge of the bench seat, fixed his eyes on William Bent's sodden buckskins and doggedly kept going. His wife, dark-haired and considered to be uncommonly attractive, resolutely kept her place next to him despite the appalling conditions. Their children were frightened by the violent rocking motion of their temporary home. Marion, the tawny-haired fourteen-year-old daughter, peered through the narrow gap at the rear and wondered just how their two milk cows were able to keep pace. She possessed a girl's sentimentality for the livestock that in reality had no place on the frontier. Gingerly, she got to her feet and made her way crab-fashion to the back. If anything happened to their animals, she intended to be there to holler out.

As Bent thankfully spotted the crossing, he reined in and scrutinized the river. The downpour, although not a purely local event, had not yet crucially affected the depth, but there was no doubt that the South Platte was flowing appreciably faster. He realized there and then that it would be too risky to pull all the men off the wagons for guard duty. The conditions were chaotic and their strength would likely be needed to control the teams of oxen. Besides, what could there possibly be to defend against in such weather?

Motioning to Chandler to keep going, he carefully eased his horse down the shallow bank and on into the water. Already soaking, he barely noticed the chill water engulfing his legs, but there was no doubting the additional vigour of the current. Nevertheless, he'd already made this crossing earlier in the day and so advanced with confidence.

Safely reaching the other side, he swung around and beckoned the lead wagon to follow him. As the oxen reluctantly plunged in, Bent watched as the other wagons followed on through the torrential rain. His attention was suddenly drawn to Jake Twelvetrees, as that man galloped madly towards the riverbank. The captain was gesticulating wildly at him, but he couldn't make out what the damned man was saying. It mattered not anyway, because Chandler's wagon was well out into the river and making good progress. The high axles and caulked wagon bed meant that those inside were able to keep remarkably dry, yet in such conditions the crossing was still fraught with anxiety.

Bent unexpectedly pondered what the hell brought these poor bastards out there anyway. All they got was danger and hardship and for what? If he'd been a more imaginative individual, it might have occurred to him that such thoughts could equally have applied to his life.

Eager to get clear of the cold water, Chandler's oxen charged up the bank and dragged his wagon safely up on to the northern side of the river. For one family at least the way was now open to continue on to Fort Laramie, but the next wagon in line had unaccountably ground to a halt on the south side. With driving rain lashing into his face, Bent enquiringly rode over to the edge. He observed

Twelvetrees bellowing forcefully at the nervous owner and in spite of the dreadful conditions a smile crept over his craggy features. That wagon master was a real 'push hard'!

The piercing scream came from behind him and took the scout completely by surprise. Wheeling his mount around in search of its source, he found himself face to face with a nightmarish scenario. Taking advantage of the appalling weather, a group of Pawnee had swept in seemingly out of nowhere and were fast approaching the solitary wagon. Marion had spotted them as she was climbing out of the back of it to check on both the cows and her father's saddle horse. Whooping with savage delight, the dozen or so warriors swiftly surrounded the Chandler's conveyance. Half of them dismounted and eagerly rushed for the undefended animals. Even as they drew their hunting knives to cut them loose, they suddenly discovered an even more valuable prize in their midst.

Panic stricken, Marion frantically attempted to get back in the wagon, but they were just too fast for her. An iron grip closed around her ankles and she was dragged, screaming out for help, away from the suddenly so welcoming opening in the canvas. Joshua Chandler appeared through the gap, brandishing an old Paterson Colt revolver, but he was terrified of hitting his daughter. Bent was far less restrained. The scout knew from experience that if the Pawnees succeeded in carrying her off, then her family might well never see her again. Dropping down from his saddle, he levelled his old 'Rocky Mountain Rifle' and drew a bead on the nearest Indian. Bracing against the expected heavy recoil, he squeezed the trigger and was rewarded with only the dispiriting pop of a percussion cap. Misfire!

'Goddamn rain!' he cursed impotently.

One of the mounted Pawnees had

observed his predicament. Howling out in triumph, the warrior galloped directly at him. In his right hand he grasped a deadly fighting axe. Bent recognized that if he was to keep his scalp he would have to move mighty fast. Reversing the grip on his long rifle, he leapt to one side and swung up at the looming savage. The solid butt caught his assailant full on in the chest and knocked him backwards off his pony. With the man temporarily winded and helpless, Bent finished him off with a tremendous blow to the skull.

Sadly, none of this brutal action benefited Marion. With a knife at her throat, her father could only watch helplessly as she was carried off to a waiting pony. The sheer horror of the girl's predicament showed in her eyes and Joshua could think of only one thing to do. 'We'll come for you,' he desperately called out. 'Whatever happens, remember that!'

The Pawnee had lost all interest in

livestock, because a white girl of breeding age who could contribute towards the longevity of the tribe was most acceptable tribute indeed. They had achieved their aim and could withdraw with honour. And yet there was one bit of unfinished business. Their friend had been killed by the buckskin-clad white man and so had to be avenged. Heavy rain might affect gunpowder, but not their more primitive weapons. Notching their arrows, four of the warriors urged their ponies towards him.

William Bent had been in some tight spots before and so he sure wasn't played out yet. Moving swiftly into cover behind his mount, he drew the two Colt Navy revolvers that he kept tucked in his belt. It might cost him the life of a valuable saddle horse, but he fully intended to survive the encounter. Cocking both weapons, he levelled them across the saddle and took rapid aim. Despite the continuing downpour, neither of his dripping Colts had actually been submerged in the river, so he prayed that at least one would discharge.

Just at that moment there came the unmistakeable crash of a Sharps rifle from a short distance behind him. One of the Indians howled with pain as the heavy ball struck him a glancing blow across the lower ribs. The gunshot mildly spooked Bent's horse, so that it shifted position just as he squeezed the triggers. By a miracle both guns fired simultaneously. Both balls went wide, but they had demonstrated his ability to fight back, so that when another revolver discharged from across the river, the Pawnees abruptly decided that it was time to cut and run. With the wounded man clinging on for dear life, they wheeled around and kicked their ponies into a gallop. Their comrades joined them with Marion slung face down over an animal's flanks and together they all disappeared back into the storm like wraiths.

Jake rode over to the scout and gazed

down at him scathingly. 'It's time you got rid of that old Hawken. It's a relic!'

'Like me, you mean,' replied Bent sharply. 'Yeah well, maybe I am too, but I'm still alive and kicking and this old rifle has served me agreeably over the years.' Patting the shoulder stock he added, 'And in case you didn't notice, it accounted for that devil over there well enough.'

It was obvious that Twelvetrees had more on his mind. 'Well anyhu, never mind the poxy gun,' responded the wagon master angrily. 'Why did you let Chandler come over without placing a guard first?'

'That river's running too fast for the wagons to be left to women and children,' Bent stated firmly. 'And that's your fault for pushing too hard!'

'Now just a goddamned minute,' snarled Jake.

That was as far as the two men got before Joshua and Martha Chandler erupted from their wagon. Already soaked, they were completely oblivious to the pouring rain. The woman was entirely inarticulate with grief, but he had plenty to say. 'Our daughter's been carried off by savages and all you two can do is argue over who's to blame. We need to go after her while they're still in the area. Can't you see that?'

None of them noticed Lee's arrival on the north bank, because the settler's voice rose to a crescendo as he swiftly continued, 'You've got to halt the train and get all the men together, now! Do you hear me? A show of force is what we need. Then those cursed heathens'll maybe give her back.' With that he suddenly fell silent as though temporarily exhausted by his tirade.

Jake and the former mountain man gazed at each other reflectively, their heated words abruptly forgotten. Both were reluctant to state the obvious and so it was left to Lee Madden to explain the harsh reality of the situation. 'I'm no Indian fighter, mister, but I have been a soldier and it seems to me that if we all go after them hell for leather, they'll just split up into small groups and double back. A wagon train full of only women and children would make a mighty tempting target and then we'd have considerably more than just your daughter to worry about! That's good guerrilla tactics and I happen to know something about such things. So if you really are going to pursue, small numbers is better.'

Chandler remained speechless for a moment longer, as though mulling over Lee's advice. Then he got his second wind. With his wife still sobbing by his side, the emotional turmoil seemed to provide him with fresh impetus. Glaring at Jake, he yelled, 'However you look at it, this is all your fault, Twelvetrees. If you'd given those devils what they wanted in the first place, they wouldn't have attacked us. And then pushing on across this river in a storm just made it easy for them. So I'm telling you plain. This wagon train is staying put until Marion is found.'

Jake's eyes became chips of ice as his

grip tightened on the Sharps rifle in his grasp. He was genuinely saddened by Chandler's loss, but no one, absolutely no one, told him how to discharge his duties. The rain was still lashing down and he was very conscious of all the other settlers waiting anxiously on the far side of the river. Dismounting, the burly wagon master squelched over until he was standing almost toe-to-toe with the enraged and grieving parent. Under the circumstances he attempted to soften his expression as he began to speak, but failed miserably.

'Chandler, I greatly sympathize with your loss, but no one family is going to delay the progress of the whole wagon train. So I'm going to get the rest of them over that goddamn river while I still can and then we're all going to move on to Fort Laramie. And if that Colt you're waving around comes anywhere near me, I'll have you clapped in irons.'

There was just no getting away from the fact that Jake Twelvetrees was one tough and ornery son of a bitch, but it was also true that Marion's capture was far from being his fault alone. As William Bent gazed at the Chandlers' grief-stricken features, he came to an abrupt decision. 'If I had held you back until Jake set a crossing guard, Marion might still be with us,' he announced regretfully. 'So I've agreed with myself that if you're up for it I'll help you get her back.'

Before the startled settler could respond, Jake barked out, 'Like hell you will! You're being paid as scout and hunter for this train until it reaches Oregon and I'll hold you to it.'

'So I resign,' remarked the other man simply.

It was Lee Madden who set the seal on events. He had remained mounted and so was able to look down on the group clustered before him. His penetrating gaze encompassed Joshua and his wife and swiftly took their measure. The husband was quite obviously no gunhand. Bent would need more support than him in any manhunt. The wife, on the other hand, was quite the most delectable creature he had seen, despite her tear-stained anxiety. It was the first time that he had observed her without a bonnet and such fine-boned features surely deserved better than the drudgery expected of a farmer's wife. That was his spontaneous opinion anyway!

Mind abruptly made up, he meaningfully placed a hand on his holstered revolver and declared, 'Reckon I'll tag along with you two. I ain't being paid for anything that I know of and I believe you'll recall that I'm too good a gun for you to try and stop me, Captain!'

Jake eyed his two employees askance. He was beginning to feel growing frustration rather than his usual impulsive anger. The downpour showed no signs of abating. He was drenched and cold and still had two score wagons to get across the South Platte. Still, he made one more effort. 'If those heathen assboils decide to sell the girl, you could end up following them clear down to Mexico. Think on that!'

'I'll take that chance,' asserted Chandler with resolute naïvety, before turning to his two volunteers. 'You have my undying thanks, gentlemen.'

'Oh Jesus,' Jake muttered cynically under his breath, but he was given no chance for further comment, because at that moment there came a loud hail from across the river.

'What would you have us do, Twelvetrees?' Rufus Barlow's sour tones were unmistakeable. 'There's more than one wagon in this train you know!'

The wagon master turned back to the river, his hackles rising again and Marion Chandler completely forgotten. 'Don't you start on me, Rufus,' he bellowed. 'Get the next in line moving. And when you're all across, I want everyone slapping axle grease on *all* the wheels!' To himself, he added, 'That'll give the bastards something to think about.'

4

Marion Chandler had known brief moments of fear in her short life, but never anything like this. Her whole being was consumed by mortal dread. With her face constantly pressed against the pony's wet flanks, the rancid smell of animal hair was overwhelming. Awkwardly bent double, she was unable to take in enough air and so an irrational terror of choking gradually beset her until she could stand it no longer. Ignoring the fact that her captor was sitting directly behind her, she suddenly reared up using all her youthful strength. Forcing her torso away from the beast, the young woman desperately sucked in a great lungful of damp night air. Sadly, the blessed relief was to be short-lived.

A savage blow struck Marion's ribs and made her cry out in pain. Unable to stop herself, she fell forward heavily against the pony. Oblivious to her discomfort, the animal remained continuously in motion under the remorseless demands of the Pawnee warrior. Even as that jolt knocked the wind from her, some form of whip lashed viciously against the back of her neck. The stinging shock elicited a howl from her sore lips and it was then that she realized the brutal truth of just how helpless she really was. With her parents quite possibly lost to her forever, these primitive creatures could do absolutely anything they wanted with her and there was nobody to stop them. As a horny hand came down proprietorially on her lower back, she began to cry pitifully.

★ ★ ★

As it turned out, her would-be rescuers did not set off in pursuit until the next morning. William Bent had affirmed that there was no point in striking out blind. Better to let the storm play itself out and then start off afresh in daylight. By then all the wagons had crossed safely and were camped on the north bank of the river. From then on they would travel parallel to the North Platte River, all the way to Fort Laramie.

The three men, greenhorn settler, mountain-man-turned-scout and soldier-turned-drifter, were still clad in wet clothes, but their weapons had all been dried and freshly greased against corrosion. Since they had no idea how long the search would take, they carried a large supply of jerked meat, pemmican and dried fruits as basic staples. Consumption of freshly cooked meat would be a luxury and only attempted if Bent was convinced that there were no hostiles in the vicinity.

'I don't know how this is going to pan out,' remarked the scout, choosing his words carefully as the three-man posse took its leave of Jake Twelvetrees. 'Hopefully we'll catch up with you before Fort Laramie, but if not, then it'll be Independence Rock. You'll be in the foothills of the Rockies by then, which will slow you down some,' he added dryly. Urging his horse forward slightly, so that he had his back to the noticeably apprehensive Joshua Chandler, Bent muttered, 'And if you don't see us there, we just ain't coming!'

The stark sight of the fallen Pawnee warrior lying untended where he had been struck down added grim weight to those words and was probably responsible for all the settlers coming to watch them leave. Nobody could be in any doubt of the danger that the three men were likely to face. Ethan Wells, whose gunshot son was slowly recovering, called out enthusiastically, 'Good luck to you, Mr Madden and thank you.'

More interestingly, so far as Lee was concerned, was the approach made by Martha Chandler. Still misty-eyed with emotion, she took his right hand and squeezed gently. 'I can't thank you enough, Mr Madden. If you help bring

Marion back to me, I'll be forever in your debt.'

He favoured her with a warm smile before silently moving away to join his two companions. In spite of that dazzling endorsement he was minded to utter a few home truths to her husband. As the three of them moved off, Lee glanced over at him and remarked, 'This is your last chance to call this off, Joshua.'

The other man appeared genuinely puzzled. 'Why ever would I want to do that? I have a son as well, of course, but Marion is the real light of my life! I would think daughters always are.'

Lee nodded grimly. 'Yeah, yeah. I don't doubt your devotion to her, but this ain't going to be anything like you're expecting. No grand charge out of the sun to rescue a damsel in distress. Some or all of us might well be mustered out without even seeing your girl.'

'So why are you coming with us, Mr Madden?'

Lee's response was chilling in its simplicity as well as being rather duplicitous. 'It seemed like a good idea. Besides, I've seen plenty of death. It holds no fear for me.'

Chandler blanched and chose to remain silent. He really couldn't think of any answer to that.

'Oh, and my name is Lee,' that man added. ''Mr Madden' has me looking for the warrant in your hand.'

★   ★   ★

They had no problem trailing the Pawnees. The ground was still soaked and the unshod ponies left a trail that even Chandler could have followed unaided. The task was made easier still when, a few miles from the wagon train, the tracks revealed that the raiding party had rejoined the main body of Indians. With the surrounding terrain remaining relentlessly flat, there was little chance of an ambush. All they had to do was make up some time and

63

thankfully their clothes were beginning to dry out in the warm sunshine.

Yet even now there were some protocols to be observed, as Bent was quick to point out. 'The trick is not to get too close too quick, because we're a mite over-matched. So long as Marion's riding double, I can keep tabs on her. The extra weight shows in the hoof prints,' he added for Chandler's benefit. 'If her new owner stays with the main band, then we're stymied. Ideally we want them to split off into smaller groups, because then we can make a move.'

Chandler gazed wide-eyed at the former mountain man. 'Do you reckon they'll be expecting us to follow them, Mr Bent?'

The scout favoured him with a genuine smile. He could happily get used to such deferential behaviour. 'Who knows? You need to be an Indian to know how an Indian thinks. They may consider that we'll accept Marion's seizure as bad luck and just continue on our way west. Or they may be hoping that we'll follow in force, so that they can swing around behind us and take another crack at the weakened wagon train.' Bent shrugged. 'But one thing's for sure and it's something you need to keep in your head. They won't kill her. She's far too valuable!'

★ ★ ★

'Well, is he with them?'

'How the hell should I know?' snarled Deacon Swain as he slammed the battered drawtube spyglass shut. 'This thing ain't worth a damn!'

'What do you expect?' responded Joe with a snigger. 'You hit that fella awful hard with it back in Kansas.'

'He was a Mormon,' Swain barked. 'He got what was coming to him.'

'And then some,' Brady added with the joy of recollection. What they had then done to the poor man with their broadswords momentarily filled him with an inner glow.

'So what are we going to do?' asked another of the gang impatiently. The sizeable wagon train stretched out temptingly before them. 'We can't ride all the way to Oregon without feeding off the fat of the land sometime you know.'

Following the murderous night-time encounter in Topeka, Swain had been pushing his six men relentlessly hard. Although he had left the vicious dispute over slavery far behind, the desire for vengeance still burned fiercely within him. His younger brother might not have amounted to much, but he had been blood kin. That was all the justification the border ruffian needed to mount a manhunt.

Since joining the so-called 'Platte River Road' they had overhauled a number of wagon trains heading west, but so far there had been no sign of their prey and in the interests of speed, Swain had not allowed any looting. Now, as he glanced around at his band of cutthroats, even he could recognize the signs of discontent that could only be ignored at his peril. Better cut them some slack, he decided, or else risk a mutiny.

'Yeah, well. Maybe we are due a breather,' he allowed. 'We'll check out this party. If Madden's not there, we'll latch on to them for a while and see what we can steal. Anything we get'll fetch good coin in Fort Laramie. And who knows, they might even have some cash money for the taking.'

His men immediately perked up at such talk. Thieving and larceny was bread and butter for such individuals and their pickings had been non-existent of late. Quite literally licking their lips, they set off in pursuit of the slow-moving wagons.

★   ★   ★

The stunning vista of Courthouse Rock had just come into view on the wagon train's right flank. Rising to an impressive 400 feet above the North

Platte Valley, the rock formation was a much-anticipated landmark for all Oregon-bound travellers. So much so that their hard-driving captain amazingly allowed them a rest stop. There was a practical reason for this of course. It was depressingly easy for a child, during a moment's gawping inattention, to stumble under a moving wagon wheel and become both a permanent cripple and a drain on their morale.

The massive formation resembled the ruins of an old castle, but for some reason the name 'Courthouse' had been applied to it as early as 1837 and that designation had stuck. With nearly all attention focused on nature's stunning attraction, it was left to the singularly unimpressed Rufus Barlow to act as lookout. And for once in his life, he actually had something useful to impart.

'Riders coming up behind us, Jake,' he bellowed down the line. 'Nobody that I recognize.' His warning contained an unmistakeable anxiety that had Twelvetrees rapidly wheeling his horse around.

The captain watched intently as the strangers trotted up to the rearmost wagon and then immediately slowed to a walk. From then on they moved steadily from wagon to wagon, blatantly perusing each of the settlers. It was as though they were searching for someone in particular. Jake was not known for being slow on the uptake and so it was that Lee Madden's mysterious arrival back in eastern Nebraska suddenly loomed large in his head. He pondered that thought for a moment and then temporarily shrugged it off as being largely irrelevant. For him, the real issue was that nobody rummaged around his wagon train without permission. So, after ensuring that his revolver was nestling loosely in its holster, he spurred his animal forward.

By sheer coincidence, the confrontation took place right next to Rufus

Barlow's wagon and because of the awesome panorama it was some time before most of the other settlers realized that something was amiss. Jake calmly reined in, so that he was directly in the path of the newcomers. His sharp eyes took in their travel-stained, brutalized features. They were obviously heavily armed, but what really caught his attention was the rolled-up tarpaulin strapped to their single packhorse. The edge of it had come loose, revealing what appeared to be a number of broadswords. So one thing was for sure; they weren't there for the scenery. His guts began to churn with apprehension, but he didn't hesitate for a moment.

'I reckon that's far enough, fellas,' he growled. 'You seem to be overdoing the simple curiosity.'

'Who's he calling simple?' whined a genuinely aggrieved Brady.

Deacon Swain completely ignored his retarded crony and settled his hard eyes on the man before him. He took in the strong, determined set to Jake's jaw and the right hand hovering close to one of Colonel Colt's more recent products. 'We were kind of hoping a friend of ours might be travelling with you,' he finally remarked softly.

Jake's response was uncompromising. 'I very much doubt that, mister. These are all decent families, heading for a new life in the west. Besides, if you're looking to search my wagon train, you've got to ask my permission . . . and then I'll tell you to go to hell!'

A shock wave seemed to pass through the gang of seven. Intimidation was their speciality and they weren't used to such a swift rebuttal. As though by pre-arrangement, those on the edges urged their animals forward, so that Jake was abruptly confronted by an encroaching semi-circle of obviously hostile gunmen.

'That's not very neighbourly of you,' Swain snarled.

'Maybe so, but then we're not neighbours are we?' Jake retorted.

'What's more, I don't really give a damn!'

The gang leader couldn't conceal his bewilderment. 'We seem to have got off on the wrong foot here, mister, but that's your choice. And for a man that's only got a bunch of witless pilgrims to back his play, you seem mighty sure of yourself.'

The wagon train captain forced his lips into a humourless smile. 'A Hawken rifle makes for a pretty good ace in the hole.'

The seven men glanced around uneasily. They could see plenty of nervous settlers watching their every move, but no sign of a hidden marksman. Then again, concealment would be the whole idea. As usual, Brady just couldn't stop himself. 'Huh, who uses a piece like that nowadays?' he crowed.

'Someone who hits exactly what he aims at,' Jake proclaimed with a masterful display of confidence. 'Now get the hell away from my wagon train or get to dying!'

Swain narrowed his eyes as he considered his options. Even one man hidden out on the plains with a Hawken muzzleloader could maybe get two of them before the rest rode him down. It really wasn't worth the risk. Far better to wait until a nightfall of their choosing and then move in hard and fast.

'Yeah, OK I'll give you this round,' he announced irritably. 'But you won't always have a sharpshooter to throw down on us.' He nodded at his men and then jerked his head away.

Jake just couldn't resist one question. 'Who did you say you were looking for?'

'I didn't,' Swain snapped back. 'But if that cockchafer Lee Madden is hiding in one of these wagon beds, then you tell him we're all thinking about him.'

Jake kept his features completely impassive, but not so Rufus Barlow. That sour-faced individual noticeably twitched as he glanced questioningly at the captain. Swain affected not to notice and merely turned his horse away, but as the seven men rode off, Jake glared angrily at the settler. 'You stupid son of a bitch. If those gun thugs weren't coming back before, then they certainly will now!'

★   ★   ★

That second night of captivity was without doubt the most terrible time that Marion had ever experienced, following as it did on a desperately unpleasant day. Since being carried off, she had spent the entire time doubled up over the back of a moving pony, like an outsize sack of grain. She had received no food or water, nor even any temporary relief from her discomfort. Her belly felt as though it had been unremittingly pummelled. She had no idea how far she had travelled or in which direction. Her only sure recollection was that shortly after being carried off, her kidnappers had been joined by a far larger party of warriors.

The constant sense of dread never left her, but having cried herself out, countless hours earlier, Marion had been reduced to the state of a numb and uncomprehending beast. So it was that when they did finally come to a halt, it was some time before she even realized it. As the last rays of light drained out of the sky, her captor remained mounted and began to repeatedly stroke her lower back and buttocks in a way that made her tremble uneasily. Another warrior called out something unintelligible in a guttural accent. Her man laughed and then without warning tipped her forward on to the grass. The wind was temporarily knocked out of her; so that all she could do was lie back and desperately suck air into her parched lungs.

Surprisingly, there was no further brutality and so Marion was eventually able to cautiously sit up and look around. To her surprise, she found

herself completely alone and unob-
served. The Pawnee warriors were
apparently more concerned with satisfying their appetites and in any case
knew that the white girl had nowhere to
run to. Whimpering slightly, she curled
up in a conscious effort to make herself
small and prayed for them to keep their
distance.

That the warriors at least intended
for Marion to survive became evident a
short time later when one of them
suddenly made straight for her. Without
a word, the strangely attired creature
tossed a gourd-like container of water
on to the ground next to her and then
followed it up with what appeared to be
a lump of meat. As the unpleasant
tasting water trickled down her throat,
she abruptly realized just how ravenous
she was. The offering looked disgust-
ingly like an outsized tongue, but she
nevertheless tentatively bit into it and to
her surprise found that it tasted
delicious.

Having rapidly consumed the meat,

she began to feel a bit bolder and so cautiously surveyed her surroundings. Her captors, belching and laughing, showed no signs of moving on and were obviously intent on settling down for the night. Although she did not know it, the fact that nothing of a sexual nature had taken place indicated that the Pawnees did not yet feel completely clear of pursuit. They preferred to get back on home territory and indulge their lusts at leisure.

The plains stretched off into the darkness on all sides and provided her with little comfort. Yet it was at that moment that Marion, fortified by food, decided that she would have to make a run for it. Something about the earlier disagreeable fondling made her think that she was far better off in the wilderness than with a pack of heathen savages. And there was always the hope that her father might just be out there looking for her as he had promised.

★　★　★

Against his better judgement, Jake Twelvetrees had agreed to fort up for the night at the base of the dominating Courthouse Rock. His natural instincts had been to continue on their journey, but the settlers had been badly spooked by the lawless appearance of Swain and his men. For some reason they found them even more intimidating than the Pawnee war party. Possibly it was because most of them had only seen the Indians at a distance and considered them to be merely inferior, primitive scavengers. As light from the cooking fires and various perforated metal 'storm lanterns' glistened off a motley selection of rifles and shotguns, some of the travellers talked big to keep their spirits up.

'Any of those sons of bitches show up here again, they'll get both barrels of this beauty!'

'This truthful Sharps'll blast those road agents all the way back to Council Bluffs!'

'If they start anything, we'll finish it

and that's no error!'

Jake sighed as he collected a plate of steaming vittles. Backing off out of the light, he found a quiet spot and settled down to eat. Those damn fools won't know what's hit them if that gang of plug uglies do show themselves, the captain decided to himself. He knew it was highly unlikely that they would return that night, if only because it was exactly what the settlers expected. Yet there was little doubt in his mind that it would happen and sooner rather than later. He just wished that the old mountain man and Lee Madden had not gone off hunting Indians. And just what have you been up to, Lee, he pondered, that's got those hornets on your tail? Something told him that, one way or another, it wouldn't be long before he found out.

5

At last Marion plucked up the courage to make her move. To a tired, fevered mind it seemed an age before her captors had finally bedded down for the night. The agonizing wait had taken its toll and she was trembling badly. So badly in fact that she was literally unable to stand up. She had never been afraid of the dark, but now every shadow contained lurking menace. Since the Indians all slept holding their ponies' reins, there would have been no possibility of stealing one even if she'd had the nerve to see it through. It was this fact that probably saved her from immediate discovery.

The only option left to her was to crawl off through the undergrowth and so, after checking yet again for any sign of movement, that was what she did. Almost immediately Marion was silently cursing her long cotton dress. Necessary to preserve her modesty, even on the frontier, it severely hampered her progress, yet gradually the young fugitive got clear. Only then did her trembles subside enough to allow her to stand up.

Knowing that she had to get as far away from the camp as possible before sunrise, Marion unbuttoned and removed her dress. Next she rolled up and knotted the single petticoat around her thighs, so as to allow more freedom of movement. Knowing full well that her pa had no money to be wasting on new clothes, she folded up her dress and clutched it tightly, as though drawing strength from something associated with her family. As a farmer's daughter, she had an affinity with the outdoors and so possessed an instinctive feeling for the direction to take. If she got it wrong, she would quite probably not live to regret it.

Drawing in a deep breath to steady her jitters, the runaway set off at a

81

steady jog. The vigorous activity served to take her mind off the desperate situation and gradually she began to calm down. Darkness on the plains is never complete, so it was comparatively easy to find a safe footfall. She was strong and well used to walking miles at a time, so for the first two hours or so she made good time. Then the cumulative effect of the ordeal itself and lack of sleep began to tell on her. Her legs started to feel leaden and her breathing became uneven. Soon only the terrible knowledge of what lay behind kept her moving at all.

★　★　★

Shortly before the first tentative approach of daylight, there was cautious movement in the cold camp on the plains. Three horses grazed contentedly on the long grass, which in itself indicated a lack of danger. Yet that didn't cut any ice with William Bent. The former mountain man knew all too well that it paid to be alert and prepared in advance of the sun's rays, because there was no telling what could be awaiting them so far from civilization. The prudent traveller would always have his weapon cocked and ready, until careful scrutiny of his surroundings calmed a fast-beating heart.

Bent was soon to discover that he was not the only one brought up to be vigilant. A few feet away, Lee Madden had his Colt Navy resting across the saddle. As the gloom slowly lifted, their eyes locked and they exchanged knowing smiles. In the background they could hear Chandler's gentle snoring, which indicated an individual most definitely unwary of life's pitfalls.

As the onset of dawn finally brought a measure of clarity to the surrounding land, they got the shock of their lives. A frightening scene was developing before their very eyes that required immediate action. A mere 200 yards away, the half-naked figure of Marion Chandler teetered on the point of collapse. Even at that distance it was obvious that she was almost done in and yet, just becoming visible on the horizon was a group a riders. Mere seconds passed before their identity became apparent.

'Goddamn Pawnees!' muttered Lee. 'And it sure ain't us they're after . . . yet.'

'Wake up, Chandler and stay down,' Bent hissed. 'Your girl's out there!'

That man jerked awake, a look of stunned disbelief on his face. 'She's alive?' he stammered. 'God be praised.'

'Yeah, but can he shoot?' queried Bent irreverently. 'Because if we don't stop them from taking her again, they might just figure she's too much trouble and finish her.' So saying, he lined up his long Hawken on the nearest warrior and drew in a steady breath. The Indians were rapidly closing on their exhausted prey, whilst she appeared completely oblivious to their presence. Even though preoccupied, it could only be scant seconds before the Pawnees noticed the white men's grazing animals.

A sudden crash split the dawn air as the powerful muzzle-loader discharged. Some 300 yards away a warrior toppled backwards off his pony and was dead before he hit the ground. As a smile of grim satisfaction crossed his features, the scout reversed his rifle and blew down the thirty-four-inch barrel prior to tipping in another powder charge.

Two things occurred as a result of that exceptional shot. Marion stopped and peered around in total bewilderment. The Pawnees uttered a collective howl of rage and made straight for the three *Taaka piita*. Joshua Chandler just couldn't contain himself. Grasping his diminutive revolver, he leapt to his feet and bellowed out, 'Marion, run to me girl. Run!'

His frantic entreaty failed in its entirety. Not only did she not dash encouragingly towards her father, she didn't even seem to have heard him.

That left only one option open to him. Entirely ignoring his two companions, the desperate man abruptly raced off across the open grassland.

'Get down, you madman,' Bent yelled, but he might as well have been addressing the man in the moon.

As the distraught settler sprinted towards his daughter, the advancing Indians swiftly reacted by splitting into two groups of five apiece. One faction swept off towards Marion, whilst the other continued its headlong charge at the two white men.

'What kind of hand is he with a belt gun?' Lee demanded.

'Probably couldn't hit a barn door, like most of them,' the scout scornfully replied as he rammed a slightly oversized lead ball down the barrel of his Hawken.

'That's what I figured,' Lee responded, as he too scrambled upright. Clutching a Colt in each hand, he trotted steadily after Chandler. His reduced speed was wholly deliberate. No one, winded from a foot race, could fire a weapon accurately.

'Jesus Christ, not you too,' complained Bent as he placed a percussion cap on to the waiting nipple and then brought the rifle up to his shoulder.

As Chandler neared his beloved offspring, he hollered out again and this time she responded. Almost absent-mindedly, Marion raised a hand in greeting and began to stagger towards him. With a pounding of hooves, the Pawnees swept up behind her. It was terrifyingly obvious that they intended to ride her down. Realizing that he had to draw them on to him, Joshua kept moving and pointed his revolver in their general direction. From behind him there came the crash of Bent's rifle and for a brief instant his spirits soared, but all the warriors immediately before him remained untouched. The scout was clearly fighting for his own scalp.

Howling out a string of obscenities, Joshua awkwardly fired on the run and kept on shooting until all five chambers in the old weapon were empty. Not one of the poorly-aimed balls struck flesh and blood. He had succeeded in drawing all their attention on to him, but in the process had rendered himself completely defenceless.

Screaming out with bloodlust, the five braves galloped directly for him, their erstwhile prisoner completely forgotten. Two of them released barbed arrows on the move and their skill was truly amazing. One arrowhead struck Joshua in his throat, whilst the other slammed into his chest. Desperately choking on his own fluids, the doomed settler abruptly dropped to his knees. His blood-spattered features registered a dreadful mixture of pain and anguish . . . anguish at the certain knowledge of never being able to hold his beloved daughter again.

Only a few yards away, Marion stared in horrified disbelief as her father toppled forward and lay twitching in his death throes. Joshua's own weight had pushed the arrow shafts through his body, so that they now gruesomely protruded from the rear. One of the warriors yelled at the grubby, sweat-stained girl in triumph and urged his horse towards her. What he was about to do would never be discovered, because at that moment the other Pawnees demanded his return. They had another white man to deal with and this one carried with him a recognizable sense of menace.

Lee Madden came to a halt and drew in deep drafts of air to steady his breathing. Fear was nibbling at his guts, but he had been in enough fights to know that it would cease once he squeezed a trigger. There were five mounted warriors facing him and he knew that he could expect no help from William Bent. That man was facing his own battle for survival and would stand or fall by his own efforts.

Only one Indian carried a firearm and he happened to be clad in the same blue US Army greatcoat with the bloodstained left breast that he had been wearing at the parley all those days earlier. Whatever the outcome, Lee determined that that man would be the first to die.

The Pawnees spread out so as to disrupt his aim. They obviously intended to overwhelm him on the first rush. A more prudent man would have dropped to the ground, but Lee's blood was up. Marion had just lost her pa for no good reason and they were surely going to pay for that.

Uttering demonic yells, the five warriors collectively surged forward. 'God save me from misfires,' he muttered before levelling his two revolvers. At fifty feet and closing, his assailants made excellent targets, just so long as he held his nerve. He triggered the right hand Colt first and then calmly aimed the other. The first discharge had blown out a small cloud of sulphurous smoke, but that failed to distract him. As 'Bluecoat' tumbled sideways from his pony, Lee fired again at another warrior and then raised both weapons to the vertical. As he cocked them, small particles of the copper percussion caps dropped out. Having minimized the risk of the guns jamming, he took rapid aim at one of the ponies and squeezed off another shot.

A .36 calibre ball ploughed agonizingly into the animal's chest, causing its forelegs to buckle. Its unfortunate rider somersaulted forward and landed on the ground with sickening force. From behind the embattled white man, another Colt Navy crashed out. William Bent was obviously still alive, but the two men might as well have been on different continents for all the good they could do each other.

Two warriors now remained mounted. One of them swiftly notched an arrow to his bow and so ensured that he was the next target for their deadly foe. Lee again aimed at the largest object and fired. The Indian had just swung broadside on and so the ball struck the pony in its flank. As blood spurted from the wound, it whinnied with pain and reared up. The barbed arrow swept past Lee's head, comfortably missing him by about three feet. The Pawnee remained mounted, but now needed all his skill just to control the wounded animal.

Lee again calmly cocked both revolvers and then with chilling deliberation began to advance on his surviving opponents. As he came level with the warrior still stunned from the heavy fall, he lowered his right hand Colt and shot him in the back of the head without even breaking step.

Such one-sided carnage proved to be too much for the surviving Indians. Both of them viciously yanked their animals around in a frantic bid to escape. The wounded pony was slowest to respond and so Lee took the time to draw a fine bead on its owner's unprotected back. He squeezed the trigger and then cursed vividly as the only result was a muted pop. Cocking the gun once more, he was about to try again when Bluecoat abruptly leapt to his feet brandishing an axe.

Lee coolly traversed the muzzle and again contracted his forefinger. This time there was a satisfying crash and the ball struck his victim full on in the face. The Pawnee fell back to the ground in a welter of blood and gore, only this time he would stay down. As the heady odour of black powder smoke wafted into his nostrils, Lee cocked both revolvers and took stock.

The two mounted warriors were out of pistol range and showed no sign of slowing. Even the one with the wounded animal was urging every ounce of speed out of the poor beast. Their three comrades were sprawled in the thick grass, all most definitely dead. Another shot rang out from the white men's campsite and this time Lee gave it his full attention. Bent had obviously been awaiting the eye contact and favoured him with the thumbs-up signal. The scout appeared to be unhurt and had apparently claimed two more victims of his own. The other three obviously recognized that their medicine had gone bad, because they were gradually retreating whilst tossing out the occasional insult. Lee discharged a ball in their direction and the enfilade fire broke any remaining resolve. The Indians turned and fled. It was only as they scurried after their compatriots that he finally turned his attention to Marion Chandler.

The grief-stricken girl was sobbing over her father's corpse, oblivious to anything around her. Lee sadly holstered his weapons and then stared intently at her for a few moments, weighing up the situation. He reflected on the injustice of Marion's mother discovering that she had permanently lost a husband whilst regaining a daughter. All he could do was help as best he could. With that in mind, he made directly for one particular slain Indian.

Glancing down at the wreckage that had been Bluecoat's face, he muttered, 'Not so tough now, are we?'

Seizing hold of the body, Lee rolled it over and roughly dragged the greatcoat free. Carrying the heavy garment over to the inconsolable girl, he stood behind her and carefully scanned his surroundings. The Pawnees had retreated out of sight, but he well knew that they had been part of a larger group.

'Marion,' he called softly. 'I know you're hurting bad, but we need to go . . . now!'

She carried on wailing over the body, her bare arms smeared with his blood. What appeared to be a rolled-up dress lay on the ground next to her. Lee chewed his bottom lip reflectively for a moment before deciding that enough was enough. If they weren't careful, that slip of a girl would end up getting them all killed.

Dropping the greatcoat, he reached down and took hold of her shoulders. Gently but firmly, he pulled her upright, away from the source of her pain. As she began to resist, he took a step back and twisted her around so that she directly faced him.

'This sounds hard, but we need to leave,' he stated insistently, but not unkindly. 'You need to fix yourself up and come with me.'

Marion's red-rimmed eyes brimmed full with tears and she simply stared at him without any sign of recognition. Lee steeled himself and then shook her hard. 'Martha sent me to bring you back,' he continued relentlessly. 'How's it going to look if you don't come?'

The girl suddenly blinked as though emerging from a trance. She momentarily peered up into his eyes and then made to turn around. Gripping her hard, Lee pulled her to him and whispered, 'There can be no looking back. It don't do any of us any good.' With that, he gently propelled her towards their camp.

William Bent viewed them speculatively. 'What a busted flush this turned out to be,' he called out drily.

'That's for Martha Chandler to

decide,' Lee responded grimly, as the pair edged closer. 'We've done what we came out here to do.'

On reaching the camp, he sat Marion down next to the scout. She was trembling badly from a combination of shock and the early morning chill, so Lee quickly retrieved the two items of clothing. Although the well-travelled greatcoat carried an evil smell, it would at least provide some real warmth. As the dazed girl slowly dressed herself, Bent nodded approvingly at his companion.

'I can see why Jake let you tag along. You're mighty handy with those belt guns.'

Lee shrugged. 'Well I say huzzah for Colonel Colt. His repeaters are the only reason we wupped those devils.'

'Huh, that and plenty of grit behind them!'

'That's as maybe,' Lee allowed. 'But there's still more than enough of them to go around out there. We need to reload and move on . . . fast! When do you reckon we'll meet up with the wagons?'

Bent cast a doubtful glance over at their youthful charge. 'She's going to slow us down some. Even so, I reckon we should cut their trail sometime after noon tomorrow, unless they've hit any problems. These heathen varmints ain't the only trouble you can encounter out here!' With that he strolled over to the nearest corpse and salvaged a bow along with a quiver of arrows. Noting Lee's quizzical glance, he smiled and remarked, 'A little keepsake. You just never know when you might need to turn silent assassin!'

6

They had made good time since leaving Courthouse Rock. With open country on all sides and no sign of any pursuit, the uneasiness of the previous night began to dissipate. Maybe those gun thugs had just taken against Jake because he was so damned ornery and had now gone on their way. That's how Rufus Barlow saw it anyhu. In his opinion it was high time that Captain Twelvetrees was taken down a peg or three.

There was one person, however, who was unable to shake off a feeling of permanent anxiety. Martha Chandler had no idea where or when her husband would reappear and she was just aching for any positive news of her daughter. She knew that Joshua was way out of his depth pursuing hostile Indians, but there had been something about that Mr Madden that inspired confidence. He seemed to possess a quiet strength that she would have found attractive, had she not been married . . . which, of course, she was. Martha felt herself colour slightly at even considering such things, but those improper thoughts had served to take her mind off Marion for a few blessed moments.

★   ★   ★

The hours drifted past without incident, as the wagon train continued on towards Fort Laramie. That place had begun to assume great importance amongst the settlers, as it represented a haven of sorts and the nearest thing to civilization that they would find in the wilderness. Before then they would have to pass two more imposing landmarks. Chimney Rock and Scotts Bluff were massive, but very different, outcrops of rock.

It was late in the evening when they

arrived at the first of the remarkable formations. Rising to nearly 300 feet, its final section clearly resembled a chimney stack and completely dominated the surrounding landscape. It was easy to see how it had received its name. Jake had more than sightseeing on his mind when he decided to make camp there, however. Parts of the vast structure's lower reaches possessed sheer sides, which would provide an ideal backstop for a defensive semicircle of wagons.

With all the animals safely inside the wooden and canvas 'walls' and the cooking fires burning, the captain carefully checked their back trail as dusk began to fall. Ethan Wells tentatively joined him, his honest ruddy features registering concern.

'You reckon they might could be still out there, Mr Twelvetrees? Only I've had Thad sat at the back of my wagon all day, watching our trail and he hasn't seen anyone.'

Jake chose to respond with a question

of his own. 'How is the lad? Will he be walking again soon?'

'Oh, he's coming on fine. He'll be hopping and skipping again afore long. Lee Madden gave out good advice and I'm grateful to him for it.'

'I kind of wish we had him here right now,' Jake remarked softly. 'Him and that mountain man both.' With that he turned away and returned to the apparent security of the wagon fort, leaving the other man to draw his own conclusions from the unsettling answer.

It had not escaped the captain's notice that nobody had so far bothered to climb on to the base sections of Chimney Rock. It was an established tradition for westward bound travellers to do so, but it seemed as though the prospect of nightfall had brought a return of their uneasiness. Rather than clambering about on one of the Platte River Road's undeniable attractions, the men folk were fingering their weapons and casting fearful glances at the lengthening shadows. One bloodless encounter with a gang of desperados had got the settlers acting like frightened sheep.

'The hell with this,' Jake muttered angrily. Collecting a plate of piping hot elk stew, he headed for the rear of the makeshift compound and then hauled himself up on to the lower reaches of the dominating landmark. Scrambling up a few paces, he found a comfortable boulder to sit on. From the splendid isolation of his perch, he contentedly scoffed the food whilst gazing out over the bivouacked wagons. Even as the light began to fail, it was obvious that the encampment was still completely alone and gradually his thoughts began to drift.

Jake hadn't realized just how far his mind had wandered, until the cold, hard muzzle of a long gun rammed into the nape of his neck. As he froze with shock, a chillingly recognizable voice called out softly, 'Don't even think of reaching for that belt gun, mister, or you won't get chance to digest them vittles.'

Keeping his hands in plain sight, Jake very slowly turned his head. There, displaying a villainous grin, was the last person that he wanted to see.

'Yeah, it's us again,' remarked Deacon Swain gleefully. 'And if your man's still out there with his Hawken, now would be the time for him to use it. Ha ha!'

Despite the churning in his guts, Jake endeavoured to keep his voice calm and level. 'I never did get your name, friend.'

'That's because I didn't give it,' replied the other man. 'Now get your ass off that rock and move over to the edge. We've got some unfinished business with you folks.' To support the demand, he jabbed his rifle barrel sharply forward.

Jake grunted with pain and got swiftly to his feet. As he did so he saw the other gun thugs surge forward around him. Cursing silently, the wagon train leader realized that they must have been waiting out of sight on the far side of Chimney Rock, which explained why no one had been on their trail.

At a nod from their leader, the motley crew abruptly dropped down into the half circle and fanned out amongst the startled settlers. Intending to utilize the last vestiges of light, Swain bellowed out across the camp from his vantage point, 'You can maybe just make out that I've got me a prisoner. Anybody pops a cap and I'll blast him.' So saying, he forced Jake over to the edge and together they dropped down off the rock. In the stunned silence that followed, Swain peered around the sea of faces until he spotted the individual that he wanted.

'You there, the sour-faced cuss. Get yourself over here, now!'

Noticeably trembling, Rufus Barlow shuffled very reluctantly towards him. There was a hunted look in the settler's eyes, as he took in the cocked weapons and belted broadswords of the seven outlaws.

'You listen good, little man,' Swain growled. 'You give me any answers I don't like and you're dead meat. Savvy?'

With beads of sweat suddenly forming on his face, Rufus nodded frantically.

'You recognized the name Lee Madden and yet I haven't seen him in the train. Just where is the son of a bitch at?'

Rufus glanced helplessly over at Jake and then peered around at the overwhelming number of settlers. He wondered why they didn't do something, before abruptly supplying Swain with the necessary answer. 'He went after a band of Pawnees. A girl was taken. He thought to get her back.'

Swain guffawed loudly. 'Very gallant. Or maybe he couldn't resist a bit of skirt, huh?'

'It wasn't like th . . . ' muttered Rufus, before the other man cut him short.

'And the sharpshooter with the Hawken. Did he even exist?'

'Oh yes,' the frightened man replied rapidly, before again glancing at Jake. 'But not when you thought. He'd already gone off with Madden and the girl's pa. They say he was a mountain man, you know. Back in the day.'

Swain glanced scornfully at the overly talkative informant. 'Do you really think I give a shit?' he snapped back, before suddenly reversing his rifle. With brutal force, he smacked the butt sharply into the back of Jake's head. As that man collapsed to his knees with a cry of pain, his assailant snarled out, 'So you thought to make a fool of me, eh?'

'Hit him again, Deacon,' cried Brady encouragingly.

'Shut up, you moron,' he responded and then did exactly that.

The second blow knocked Jake insensible and sent him face down on to the grass. Swain swaggered nonchalantly past him, his thoughts now on other matters. Gazing speculatively at the wagons, he began to think aloud. 'So whether Madden makes it back to you fine people depends on how he fares with the Pawnee. Huh, well that's just dandy. After all this and we might not even get to see him bleed.' Spitting in the dust, he muttered, 'I reckon we need some compensation for our disappointment.'

His men waited expectantly as he came to a decision. Nodding his head, he suddenly barked out, 'We've got a little business to conduct, so all you pilgrims are going to drop your firearms, now!'

The settlers had overwhelming superiority of numbers, but that really didn't count for much. There would always be a vast difference between shooting snakes and facing up to a cold-eyed killer with a gun in his hand. All seven marauders had that look and that gave them a decisive edge. Sheepishly, every man in the wagon train laid down his weapon . . . with one crucial exception.

'Now that wasn't so hard, was it?' crowed Swain exultantly. 'Now me and my men owe it to ourselves to live high for a while and you all are going to give us the means. But, we're going to be reasonable. We're not going to skin you. We just want a contribution from everybody. Freely given, of course. Ha ha ha.' Waving his men forward, he added, 'Help yourselves, boys. These good people aren't going to give us any trouble.'

Hooting and hollering, the border ruffians swooped on the settlers like locusts. Coins, fob watches, rings and even a little jewellery were collected, but the men were still careful not to lower their guard. Their guns remained cocked and levelled as they gleefully pocketed the ill-gotten gains. Swain knew that the travellers were only surrendering those items closest to hand, but that was all right. If things panned out as he expected, he and his men would take another crack at the luckless wagon train out beyond Fort Laramie, when there would be no prospect of aid from any quarter. Because by then, one way or another, Lee Madden would be crow bait and they could return to Kansas with bulging pockets.

It was a roughneck named Joe that introduced a much darker tone to the situation. He contentedly 'trousered' all that came his way, until he reached Martha Chandler. His watery eyes bulged as he took in her lush figure and fine features.

'Well lookee here,' he announced lustfully. 'Ain't she a peach? Forget all this other junk. She's the real prize and she's coming with me!'

Martha stared in wide-eyed horror at the loathsome thug. She was all too aware that she had no husband to protect her and in truth he probably wouldn't have been able to anyway, but she had no intention of going quietly. 'Well isn't anyone going to stop them?' she demanded of her companions.

There was a stunned silence as all the men folk eyed their discarded weapons, but no one made a move.

'I am,' asserted Jake Twelvetrees, drawing his revolver. Unnoticed by anyone, he had got to his feet behind Swain's men. Blood trickled from his scalp and he was clearly shaken, but there could be no doubting his determination. As Joe swung around in surprise, Jake took rapid aim and fired. The sudden gunshot stunned everyone and no more so than his victim.

The ball struck Joe squarely in his chest and rocked him back on his heels. Surprise turned to horrified shock as he looked down at the blood pumping from his body. 'I'm murdered!' he moaned dismally, before crumpling to the ground.

Jake staggered slightly as he switched to another target and that hesitation was all his opponents needed. Swain's rifle and two other revolvers crashed out in unison. All three balls slammed into their victim, snuffing out his life in an instant. As Captain Twelvetree's broken body slumped to the ground, one of the women emitted a piercing scream. It seemed to hang in the air for a long moment and then abruptly tailed off.

The six remaining gunmen instinctively herded together, their weapons covering the shocked settlers. For a brief time it appeared as though absolute paralysis had set in. Then, from around the lurking shadows of the makeshift compound, a growl of anger went up. The brutal slaying of their feisty leader had finally aroused the peaceful overlanders. Some of them hidden at the rear bent down to recover their weapons.

Deacon Swain was no fool. He recognized the possibility of an unwanted bloodbath that could quite likely take him down. 'Keep back, you dogs,' he bayed. 'I'll muster out anyone that moves!' After allowing his belligerent words to sink in, he then added in a far softer tone, 'Right then,

I reckon we'll be leaving you now . . . without the woman.'

Cautiously the six men backed off towards the massive rock. They made no attempt to recover the body of their companion. To men like them, 'dead was dead'.

As the marauders retreated into the night, Martha was the first to find her voice. 'Damn you, Rufus Barlow. You brought all this on us. It's thanks to you that Jake's lying there in the dirt.'

There was muttered agreement around the camp, but Rufus came back swiftly now that his life was no longer in danger. 'It's Lee Madden you should be accusing. 'Twas him that brought them down on us.'

'Right now, it matters not who's to blame,' protested Ethan Wells as he sadly regarded the bloodied corpse of their fallen leader. 'We're out here in the middle of nowhere and we don't even know the way!'

★   ★   ★

It was late in the following afternoon when the three riders located the wagon train.

'Something sure ain't right,' remarked William Bent immediately. The wagons no longer held to the tight formation of old and were spread out over a far greater distance. There appeared to be an unusual lethargy amongst the settlers as they plodded alongside.

Lee Madden was riding double with Marion, as he had been all day. Since leaving the killing ground, she had literally clung to him like a leech and refused to ride alone. Following the scout's line of sight, Lee could only agree with him. 'Jake must have gone down with the Bloody Flux or something, to have let discipline slip like that.'

Leading Joshua's horse, they surged forward to make themselves known.

★　★　★

That day proved to be both the best and worst of Martha Chandler's life.

Watching the reduced rescue party return with Marion apparently unharmed, her mind turned somersaults. Then, as she clung to her sobbing daughter, the horrendous reality dawned on her. Her precious Marion had been returned to her, but the Chandler family no longer possessed either a father or husband.

'All I can say, ma'am,' declared Lee hesitantly, 'is that Joshua died saving his child. I know it's cold comfort, but he fought well and didn't suffer . . . overmuch. I'll take my leave now, but if there's anything I can do, just ask.' With that, he gratefully backed off. The woman had some grieving to do and he needed to hear about the death of his friend. Consequently, as he strode away from the Chandler wagon, he had no idea that Martha was watching him intently. She was listening as Marion tearfully related the events of her rescue and, in spite of the tragic turn of events, it made quite a story!

★   ★   ★

'You left Jake's body to the buzzards. Is that how little you thought of him?' Lee was almost beside himself with anger as he viewed the assembled settlers. Under his unrelenting gaze, they shuffled about uncomfortably. William Bent stood silently by as he waited to see the outcome of the confrontation.

It was Ethan Wells that finally came up with a response of sorts. 'We figured it best to get clear of that place. We laid him out next to the man he'd killed. There seemed to be some justice in that.'

'Huh, I couldn't give a rat's ass about the scum he paroled to Jesus. I just know that *my* captain at least deserves a decent burial and that's what he's going to get.' Lee glanced over at the scout and his expression softened. 'I'm going to Chimney Rock to do the necessary. When I've finished there I'll come on after you. That's if these folks still want my company, of course.'

Rufus's jaw began to work, but he wasn't given the chance to comment.

Martha Chandler, still tightly clutching her daughter, had come up behind the assembly. There could be no doubting her opinion. 'This man helped bring Marion back to me. If needs be I'll cover his keep all the way to Oregon and you won't have any say in it, Rufus Barlow!'

It was William Bent that sealed matters. 'With Captain Twelvetrees gone, we're going to need all the help we can get if this wagon train is to get over the Rockies and beyond. We don't know who all else we're going to bump up against out there and this fella handles a brace of Colts better than I've ever seen. So do what you need to and come back to us, Lee.' With that, he chuckled and slapped a solid thigh. 'I could get used to this. I might just hire myself on as a wagon captain next spring. Now let's get those wagons moving, people and put a spring in your step. We're burning daylight!'

Lee turned away to retrieve his horse, but as he did so his eyes came to rest on those of Martha Chandler. Their glances locked and held for what seemed an awful long time, before finally he smiled and broke off the contact. It occurred to him that there really had to be some truth in the old saying, 'every cloud has a silver lining'. And if that wording wasn't quite correct, well then it would certainly do for him!

7

First Lieutenant Hugh Fleming squirmed uncomfortably in his regulation blue frock coat as he walked across Fort Laramie's parade ground. The afternoon was beginning to generate some real heat, which might have been welcome had he been enjoying a picnic on the banks of the Laramie River. As it was, the young officer was embroiled in matters of discipline with various enlisted men and had stepped out of the post's headquarters' building to clear his head.

Reaching the nearest building, Fleming ducked around the side of it into the shade and thankfully lit a cheroot. Luxuriously drawing in a deep draught of tobacco smoke, he idly gazed off to the east. Beyond the clutch of tepees pitched by the 'tame' redskins that habitually congregated around the fort, he glimpsed a group of travellers approaching. Something about their appearance attracted more than casual attention. Half a dozen in number and quite obviously armed to the teeth, they led a packhorse and one empty saddle horse. That in itself begged a number of questions. Where was the animal's owner? Had he fallen an innocent victim to one of the many predators on the northern plains or had the newcomers stolen it from someone outside of their party?

One thing was for sure. Lieutenant Fleming had been out on the frontier long enough to recognize trouble when he saw it and they reeked of it with a capital T. It was an unfortunate fact of life that since the discovery of gold in California, every ruffian and opportunist under the sun had been heading west. He decided there and then to visit the fort's trading post before he returned to his duties. It behoved him to pass on a warning to its owner, James Bourdeau, as that individual would most certainly encounter the visitors.

Had he known of the events that had occurred some days earlier, he would have had no hesitation in calling out the guard. As it was, Deacon Swain and his cronies were free to spend their recently acquired booty, secure in the knowledge that their victims were well behind them.

★　★　★

The wagon train had just passed Scotts Bluff when Lee caught up with it. He had been so engrossed in his own thoughts that he had barely given the massive rock formation a second glance. The awful sight of Jake Twelvetree's lifeless body had made him realize that fleeing westward had been a big mistake. He had thought that by doing so he could avoid more bloodshed, but it was obvious that for some people there was just no forgetting.

As he overhauled each wagon, he acknowledged the greetings from those that chose to offer them. The story of his fight with the Pawnees had evidently got about, because he noticed that a number of the men now viewed him with a new respect. Finally he reached the lead wagon. Martha Chandler was walking easily alongside of it with her young son, Samuel and occasionally flicking a light whip at the team of labouring oxen. Of Marion there was no sign and he could only presume that the girl was still resting inside after her ordeal.

As he drew level, Martha looked up at him. The widow was wearing a very plain and practical cotton smock, but even that could not subdue her natural beauty. She favoured him with a delicious smile that abruptly filled him with a warm glow. It was suddenly his earnest preference to dismount there and then, but he knew that he had better have words with Bent first. With a friendly wave, he reluctantly spurred his horse forward, unwittingly leaving her puzzled and slightly anxious. Was that all that she was going to see of him?

'Didn't think you'd manage those last few yards,' the scout remarked drolly. 'But I'm right glad to see you back. I take it you said some words over Jake?'

Lee's expression was suddenly grim. 'I did.' He hesitated slightly, before adding. 'And they included a promise to see justice done, one way or another!'

Bent regarded him intently for a few moments, as though making his mind up over something. 'I don't normally favour prying into another man's business, but your past seems to have caught up with all of us. Wells tells me that those varmints intend coming to conclusions with you, so I'd take it kindly if you'd . . . '

Lee's features were noticeably pale and drawn as he interrupted. 'It's about a feud between two families, but you can mark my words that it'll end up as a war between the states afore long.'

Bent's eyes widened at such a

sweeping statement, but he held his tongue. There was obviously far more to come.

'I'd never paid much heed to the rights or wrongs of slavery. Such high-minded thoughts were for other people and I was too busy looking after what was mine, I guess. After the Mexican War ended, I bought a farm in Kansas and settled down with a fine woman. Lisa was her name. She was all I could have wanted and then some.' He stopped briefly as a slight tremor attacked his right eye. 'We'd heard about the unrest in other parts of the territory, but never thought it would touch us. Then one night a gang of pro-slavery thugs led by Deacon Swain's brother, Usaph, fetched up at our spread. There was some wild shooting and my barn was set afire. After the dust settled I looked around for my Lisa.'

Tears welled up in Lee's eyes as he briefly struggled with his emotions. 'A stray ball had taken her in the throat.

She'd died before I even knew it. After that the farm went to ruin. All I cared about was revenge. My brother and cousins came in with me when I went after the Swains. I had picked up some lethal skills in the war and there were many bad things done. Finally, I sort of came to my senses. I realized that if the violence was ever to end, I would have to leave the territory.'

He blinked rapidly, as though coming out of a bad dream and suddenly settled his gaze on William Bent. 'Burying my old comrade, Jake, proved that it wasn't over . . . yet. What really worries me is just how Deacon found out where I had gone. It's a huge country. I should have been able to get lost easily, unless he made someone talk.'

The scout had absorbed all that he had heard and was quick to respond. 'So there's to be some more killing then?'

Lee nodded with bleak determination. 'I think that there must be. Which is why it might be better if I was to leave this train.'

Bent shook his head adamantly. 'The way I see it, those pus weasels intend coming back for seconds anyway, once we're clear of the fort. There's no law up in the Rockies, so it won't matter how many they kill. I saw how you handled those Pawnees. I reckon we're a sight better off with you than without you.' He hesitated briefly, before winking broadly. 'And there's a young widow back there who's going to need help if she's to keep her wagon on point. There's been mutterings already that she should move back down the line. Without a man by her side, I can't rightly refuse them.'

Lee's expression brightened. 'Well if you put it like that, I suppose I might could see my way to help her out . . . at least until we reach Fort Laramie.'

Bent chuckled. 'Yeah, right,' he remarked and then quickly wheeled his mount away before the other man could respond.

* ★ *

Martha Chandler peered out from beneath the wide brim of her hat and sighed with relief as she watched Mr Madden turn his horse towards her wagon. Although only very recently bereaved, she was enough of a pragmatist to know that she needed help. Handling the day-to-day demands of the journey was tough enough, but on top of that she had to cope with a traumatized daughter, her own grief and that of a son for his pa. The only saving grace was the fact that Marion had managed to escape her captors before being 'utterly degraded' by one or all of them. That meant that she at least stood a good chance of obtaining a very necessary husband once they arrived in the Oregon Territory.

As Lee pulled his horse alongside to match her walking pace, Martha glanced up at him. She was taken aback to notice that he appeared to be temporarily tongue tied and even shy.

Not at all what she expected from a 'killer of men', but somehow it only seemed to increase his appeal. She did not take to pushy braggarts. Sweeping some stray hair away from her sweat-stained forehead, she proffered a gentle smile and made a start at some conversation. 'I don't think I'll ever get used to the total emptiness of this land, Mr Madden. It's like nothing I've ever seen before and just seems to go on and on for ever.'

'You obviously haven't seen my farm in Kansas,' he remarked dryly, but then favoured her with a broad smile that lit up his strong features. The ice was broken and he intended to make the best of it. 'It's the lack of good timber that's hardest to take. It doesn't seem right, building a house out of clumps of earth. Oh, and my friends call me Lee.'

Dismounting, he hesitantly cleared his throat before continuing. 'I'd take it kindly if you'd allow me to tie my horse off on the back of your wagon. That way I'd be free to help out . . . if you should need me that is.'

Martha laughed out loud for the first time in many days. 'I think I might allow you that small indulgence ... Lee.'

Myriad thoughts went through Lee's mind as he led his animal to the back of the swaying conveyance. 'Indulgence' was a four-dollar word in his book and her use of it indicated both schooling and intelligence. That would have doubtless aggravated some men, but he found it rather appealing. Beauty and brains. What more could a man want? And yet his next action would mark a serious turning point. Attaching his belongings to her wagon showed his intentions for all to see and her apparent acceptance of them. He'd better be damn certain that he was doing the right thing.

Glancing back down the train, he noticed that the occupants of the next wagon in line were watching him intently. He stared straight at them for a moment and suddenly his mind was made up. Looping the reins through a cast-iron ringbolt, he casually touched his hat brim in a mock salute and turned away. One thing was for sure; he knew how to handle them and any other busybodies that took too close an interest in his affairs and he felt sure that they realized it.

As he rejoined the woman and her silent son, it was obvious that she had something specific to say. After instructing Samuel to go clear some large stones out of the path of the advancing wagon, she moved closer until there was barely a hair's breadth between them.

'First off, I want to thank you for the life of my child. I owe you a debt that I can never repay.'

He made to respond, but she held her hand up. There was much more to come. 'We barely know each other,' she quietly continued. 'Therefore I'm going to speak plainly, so that there can be no misunderstandings. Joshua was a good man, but my feelings for him stopped short of love. The marriage was arranged by our two families before I had reached an age to prevent it. Over time we did grow closer and having the children helped, but deep down, he knew that relations could have been better between us and that and other matters gnawed on him. For one thing, he couldn't seem to move out of his pa's shadow. Moving out to Oregon seemed a way to prove that he could make something of himself, but that meant that we had to accompany him on this journey and in the end it . . . it killed him.'

Martha abruptly stopped both talking and walking and gestured back down the line of wagons. 'If I could turn back I would, but it's too late for that. Yet Mr Bent says that I can't cross the high reaches without help and I sense that you're a decent man. So if you want to join me for the journey, you're welcome. What's ours will be yours, but you'll sleep outside of the wagon until told otherwise!' With that she suddenly picked up the pace to rejoin her wagon.

Lee couldn't contain himself. 'Ha, you sure tell it like you see it, don't you?'

She made no comment and so on impulse he stuck out his right hand, giving her no option other than to take it. As her firm, but definitely female grip enclosed his, he added, 'Well OK then, Martha. We have an agreement. It'll be our own little treaty. We'll just have to make sure that it works out better than most of those signed by governments.'

Martha peered up at him curiously, so he smiled and added, 'Yeah, I got in some schooling as well.'

★   ★   ★

The moment William Bent announced that the wisps of smoke he had spotted came from Fort Laramie, great whoops of joy rippled down the line of wagons. After long arduous weeks of plodding through what was to them a desolate wilderness, the prospect of resting up in relative safety held great appeal. For the next few days, the weary travellers would be under the protection of G Company of the United States 6th Infantry and they couldn't wait to get there.

Suddenly reinvigorated, they urged the teams on to greater efforts and yet the sun had long passed its zenith by the time they actually saw some buildings. Surely nobody could feel guilty at ending the trek early that day? Hell, even Rufus Barlow had a smile on his face; the first anybody could remember since leaving Independence, Missouri.

Bent led them wide of the native encampments and on to the area of lush grass reserved for white settlers. This stretched between the fort and the point where the Laramie River ran into the North Platte. The oxen would need plenty of good grazing to rebuild their strength after the long haul. The overlanders wheeled the wagons around in a wide circle, mainly to keep their stock contained rather than as a defensive measure.

Lee was keen to get into the fort, but not for the same reason as everyone else. Touching Martha companionably on the arm, he announced, 'While you all get situated, I'm going to visit the post commander. I want to know if Swain's crew have been through here. These folks may have forgotten all about Jake Twelvetrees, but I sure haven't.'

As he walked off, he realized that he had been overly harsh in his criticism and he knew exactly why. In truth, he was feeling guilty at the lack of thought he had given his former captain over the last few days. The distraction of female company had been very pleasant indeed and made him appreciate just how much he had missed it. Even Marion had started to come round after her experiences and seemed to feel a special bond towards her saviour.

★ ★ ★

The post headquarters was like so many other buildings allocated to the frontier army. Fly blown, hastily constructed and poorly ventilated. Without a major war to contend with, the United States Congress was notably reluctant to lavish funds on its overstretched armed forces. The office's prime occupant was Lieutenant Fleming and that grandly moustachioed individual was feeling harassed.

'Yeah, they were here all right. Created all kinds of hell and then left in a hurry.'

Lee briefly described the crimes committed on the trail. 'So it would help if we knew where they were headed.'

The young officer favoured him with a keen glance. 'Why don't you ask one of them? I've got him locked up in the guardhouse.'

Lee was flabbergasted. 'On what charge?'

'That depends on whether Bourdeau's man survives. He's a French Canadian who runs the trading post here. One of his employees took the serrated blade of a hunting knife in his guts. That said, if the prisoner had anything to do with killing your man, I'll go right ahead and hang him for that murder anyway!'

With a fire suddenly burning in his belly, Lee followed Fleming out of the office and over to the guardhouse. His eyes gleamed with eager anticipation. To have Deacon Swain already under lock and key would change everything. As it turned out, only one of the three cells was occupied and it required only a brief glance at its single inmate to provoke crushing disappointment. Scrawny, pockmarked and heavily bruised, his features were completely unfamiliar even under further careful scrutiny.

'Bourdeau gave him quite a battering,' remarked the lieutenant with obvious satisfaction.

'Do you know who I am?' Lee rasped angrily.

The prisoner gazed at him with total disdain. 'Looking at me in here, do you think I give a shit?'

Lee's eyes narrowed ominously as he closed in on the cell. 'You might when you're hopping and squealing at the end of a rope,' he countered softly.

'For what?' the other man sneered. 'Knifing that cockchafer was self-defence. He'd watered the whiskey down and then threatened me when I complained.'

'All six of you felt threatened?' scoffed the army officer.

'You can't be too careful, General. I hear tell there's some real bad hombres out on the frontier,' responded the prisoner in a pitiful attempt at blameless naïvety.

Lee turned away scornfully. 'I don't recognize this piece of trash, Lieutenant. I'll have to get some of the settlers in here to look him over. They'll tell you if he was one of the three at Chimney

Rock that pulled a trigger.'

The blue-coated officer nodded indulgently. 'Fair enough, Mr Madden. Their sworn affidavits will be enough to condemn him.'

From inside the cell, there was a hacking cough followed by a shuffling noise as the prisoner got to his feet. 'Lee Madden,' the man hissed. 'So you're the one Deacon's so keen to kill.'

'He'll get his chance,' Lee calmly retorted. 'Why don't you do yourself a favour and tell us his plans? That way, if you didn't actually kill Jake, it may encourage the lieutenant to reduce your sentence.'

'Huh. If I rat Deacon out, I'm dead for sure. Just like that poxy brother of yours in Topeka.'

A great chill came over Lee and for a few moments he was completely unable to speak. His hands began to tremble uncontrollably and so in an effort to steady them he advanced to the cell's iron bars and took a tight hold. Despite the barrier, the wretch before him nervously took a rapid step back.

'Which one of you vermin killed Liam?' Lee bellowed, almost beside himself with rage.

Belatedly realizing that the locked cell kept people out as well as in, the prisoner recovered some of his nerve. 'Was that his name?' he taunted. 'Well, no matter. You wouldn't recognize him now, anyway. Those soft lead balls make a hell of a mess, ha ha.'

Lee howled out in anguish and grabbed one of his revolvers. His tormenter's courage abruptly vanished and that man leapt backwards, all the while staring imploringly at the infantry officer. As the Colt Navy ascended through the bars, the soldier grabbed Lee's arm and yanked him backwards. 'This is an army post, Mr Madden,' he barked. 'There'll be no cold-blooded murder here.' With that, he gestured for the sentry to usher the suddenly troublesome civilian out of the room.

Stubbornly holding his ground, Lee barked out at the occupant of the cell,

'What's your name, you scum-sucking piece of trash?'

'Go to hell! It weren't me that did for your brother and you can't prove it was.'

At that point, the sentry none too gently pushed him back with the barrel of his Springfield rifle. Lee reluctantly retreated under the pressure and soon found himself outside, to be shortly joined by the lieutenant. Regarding him suspiciously, Fleming quickly spoke his mind.

'Seems to me you've brought your own private war west with you, Mr Madden. What happened in Kansas is no concern of mine. You're welcome to send some of your party over to identify the prisoner, but if he didn't actually kill Twelvetrees he'll have to answer for his bad deeds in the trading post instead. Gutting somebody with a knife is more serious than robbery. Oh and I'd be obliged if you'd keep clear of the guardhouse from now on. If that wretch is to die, it won't be by your hand.'

Lee struggled to contain his temper as he responded. 'Doesn't it matter to you that Jake Twelvetrees served under Winfield Scott in the Mexican War? In fact so did I. I was a lieutenant just like you. That must count for something.'

Fleming registered surprise and his expression softened slightly. 'In that case, I'm truly sorry for what has happened . . . to both of you, but my duty is clear. That man will be punished, but not by a vigilante. Good day to you, sir.' With that, the soldier turned and walked back to his office without a backward glance.

It was at that point that Lee made a solemn vow. One way or another, when the wagon train left Fort Laramie, Swain's thug would be in a cold hole in the ground!

8

For Lee Madden, the following ten days were an uncomfortable mixture of frustration and pleasure. The latter emotion was due in no small part to his association with Martha Chandler. Released from the grinding toil of the journey, all the settlers were initially light-headedly carefree and even she no longer seemed to be unduly troubled over the loss of her husband. Lee helped with the chores and took a genuine interest in her children, so that his attendance in and around the wagon became almost expected. And yet, he was never able to completely relax and she was shrewd enough to recognize it. However, since he had not told her all that had transpired in the guardhouse, she suspected that his reticence was due to the fear of making some form of commitment.

Towards the end of their stay, the visitors found out the cost of restocking with essentials so far from home and the fort's artificial glow abruptly faded.

'It's no wonder Bourdeau's man got stabbed,' growled Rufus Barlow angrily. 'Using his store is worse than getting held up by road agents. What they need here is some competition.'

Lee's main problem with that first statement was that 'stabbed' had not become 'murdered'. By some miracle, completely unrelated to the primitive care that he had received, the trading post's employee had survived the vicious assault. Compounding that unexpected turn of events, a group of settlers had visited the guardhouse and reluctantly cleared the prisoner of actually killing Captain Twelvetrees. Therefore, the most that he could be charged with was assault and robbery, neither of which was a hanging offence as no horses had been taken.

'You just watch,' remarked William Bent with frightening prescience. 'The next time you see that son of a bitch, he'll be in uniform. Because, as you well know, the army'll take anyone. And then, some dark night he'll up and desert. You just see if he doesn't.'

Lee gently took the grizzled scout by an arm and led him out of earshot of the others. 'You intend that we move on tomorrow, don't you?'

Bent nodded emphatically. 'Animals and humans both are well fattened up. The laundry's done, the provisions are in and the Rockies need crossing. So yeah, tomorrow at sun up we're leaving the delights of Fort Laramie behind.' He suddenly eyed Lee warily. 'Why? Just what are you thinking on?'

'I'm going to need the bow and arrows that you brought back with you.'

The former mountain man caught on immediately. 'Just leave it alone, Lee. No good will come of killing that bull turd. You'll just end up in the damn guardhouse yourself.'

'My mind's made up, Will. By his own admission he had a hand in killing my brother. The bastard even laughed about it! Could you let that go if it was your kin?'

Bent regarded him stonily for a few moments, before reluctantly shaking his head. 'No . . . No, I guess not. Come see me after dark. Meantime you'd better go say a few words to that widow woman you've been shadowing. She deserves more than you just disappearing into thin air.'

★　★　★

Martha Chandler watched carefully as Lee walked towards her. There was something about his measured tread and set expression that alerted her to not expect small talk. Which was a shame, because she increasingly found herself looking forward to his company and his presence around the wagon was definitely helping her children to adjust to the death of their father. In truth she was becoming attracted to him, which could be a problem when they reached

Oregon if he turned out to be just another rootless drifter, like so many single men heading west. And yet . . . there was an obvious decency to him that gave her hope for the future.

Lee favoured her with a searching glance, before launching nervously into his hastily prepared speech. 'I'll very likely have to take off kind of sudden tonight, but there'll be a good reason for it, so don't you go thinking otherwise. The simple fact is, I aim to have a reckoning with that sorry cuss in the guardhouse. Trouble is, if that prissy lieutenant decides to pursue me, I may have to keep clear of the wagon train for a while.'

Martha was plainly shocked. 'I know Jake was your friend, but is that worth becoming a fugitive?'

Lee couldn't help himself. He stepped closer and took her hand. 'It's more than that. Those road agents also killed my brother, Liam, back in Topeka, so they all have to pay. I just wanted to tell you that I have glimpsed happiness again these last few days. I *will* come back, so long as the thought of another killing doesn't give you pause.'

He had given her a lot to think about, but the doubt on her features was barely a flicker and then it was gone. 'The Indians that you shot had killed Joshua and kidnapped my daughter. They had it coming and I suppose the man held by the army has too. After all, he robbed us and stabbed that trader.' She paused and squeezed his hand firmly. 'So you do what you have to, Lee Madden, and then come back to us in one piece.'

Knowing that he couldn't have dared hope for a better response, he felt a tremendous warmth well up inside. One way or another he was going to justify her faith in him.

* * *

Although buoyed by optimism, it still seemed to take an age before darkness finally fell. Only then did Lee make his way over to the scout's bivouac. He found Bent waiting for him with a rolled-up blanket and rather more bizarrely, a tin plate.

'The bow and arrows are inside,' he offered by way of explanation. 'And when I plonk some piping hot beans on the plate, you've got food for the prisoner. Whether he gets to enjoy a last supper will be up to you,' he added drily.

Lee was both surprised and grateful. Bent had obviously given some thought to the deadly scheme, but that man had no interest in gratitude. Waving away the other's thanks, he said, 'Go and get it done. When you feel it's safe to rejoin the train, I'll be glad to see you. It ain't easy doing both my job and Jake's.' With that he produced a pan of beans from his campfire and slopped a generous helping on to the plate. 'Have fun,' he chuckled before turning away.

*   *   *

On the far side of the fort, the campfires of the agency Indians burned brightly, but inside the cordon of buildings the guardhouse was in almost total darkness. Conveniently for Lee, the adobe structure was situated well away from the barracks and other buildings that were likely to be heavily inhabited. Even so, he remained in the shadows of the nearby stable block for some considerable time as he carefully scrutinized the interior of the fort. What guards there were, naturally seemed to be more interested in the activity outside. After all, the wagon train contained women, a commodity that was in painfully short supply on the frontier.

Finally he made his move. Clutching the rolled-up blanket and plate of beans, the would-be assassin swiftly approached the guardhouse. He had no idea whether the door was locked or not and really didn't care. What mattered was having the guard where he wanted him. Drawing in a deep breath, he rapped sharply on the door.

There was a brief pause before a disorientated voice called out, 'Who is it?'

Realizing that he had caught the man asleep, Lee officiously replied, 'Food for the prisoner. Open up, this plate's hot!'

'Which prisoner?' queried the guard peevishly.

Lee jerked with surprise. Which prisoner? he pondered. That means there's more than one. Yet there could be no turning back and he knew that it was crucial to maintain momentum. 'Who gives a shit which one? Food's food. Just open the goddamn door!'

There was the reluctant shuffling of feet as the guard finally made a move. He hadn't recognized the voice and so couldn't be sure just what rank he was up against. Lee heard a metallic noise as a key turned in the lock.

'I hope you've brought me something,' the soldier muttered plaintively. 'I've been fastened up in here for hours and everybody seems to forget about me.'

As the door swung open, his visitor announced, 'It's all yours,' and launched himself forward. With perfect timing, the still-hot beans landed squarely in the guard's face. Howling with pain and surprise, he staggered back. His rifle fell to the floor, as both hands grabbed at the glutinous food. Lee stepped rapidly to one side and brought the butt of his revolver down sharply on an unprotected head. With a grunt, his victim collapsed heavily to the floor without even having seen his assailant. Lee holstered his Colt and carefully closed the door.

'Who the hell are you?' demanded a familiar voice.

Lee turned to face the cell and as he did so, light from an oil lamp illuminated his features.

'Sweet Jesus,' hissed the scrawny prisoner. 'Just what are you about?'

Lee momentarily ignored him and peered into the next cell. His heart sank at the sight of a blue uniform. The hastily conceived plan had counted on the single inmate being skewered by a Pawnee arrow, thereby leaving his involvement as suspected but unproven. The presence of another prisoner changed everything. His stark choice was to either 'cut and run' and be wanted for assault, or finish what he had started in front of a witness whose testimony could surely hang him.

'What are you in here for?' Lee demanded of the soldier.

'Drunk in charge,' replied that man in the sort of tone that suggested he still was.

'Goddamn it all,' Lee snarled back. 'You picked a hell of a time to hit the joy juice, Private!' Then abruptly his mind was made up and he unfurled the blanket. It was still worth using the Pawnee's weapon, if only to avoid the sound of a gunshot. Swain's man suddenly had eyes like saucers as he saw the bow and arrows.

'Just what are you fixing to do with

those?' he queried with obvious unease.

Lee notched one of the arrows. 'You never did tell me your name, you little runt.'

'What's it to you anyway?' that man responded with forced belligerence.

'Somebody will need to know what to put on your marker,' Lee replied as he drew back the gut bowstring. Advancing with chilling deliberation, he took careful aim between the bars.

'Sweet Jesus. You're mad,' the prisoner exclaimed as he looked desperately about for any form of protection. Leaping for his flimsy wooden cot, he frantically dragged it upright and swung it in front of him in the form of a shield. The soldier in the next cell regarded the unfolding drama with bewilderment, before blowing air through his lips like a horse and unexpectedly passing out.

'If only he'd done that earlier,' Lee remarked bitterly as he lined the arrow up at his victim's torso. His arm trembled ever so slightly. It's a hell of a thing to kill a man in cold blood and for him it would be a first. He could feel beads of sweat forming on his forehead and his hands were suddenly clammy. If he was going to go through with it, it had to be now.

It suddenly occurred to that terrified individual to hold the wooden barrier out in front to maybe absorb most of the projectile, but he was just too late. As the bowstring was released at point-blank range, the iron-tipped arrow plunged into and through the fragile barricade before slicing into skin and muscle tissue. With a strangled cry, the border ruffian released his hold on the cot. Desperately seizing the primitive weapon that protruded from his chest, he tried to heave it back out, but already his strength was failing. Hands greasy with blood, all he succeeded in doing was to highlight his bizarre predicament.

Part of the arrow was still wedged in the thin timber, so that he was effectively shackled to it. By letting go of it, the mortally wounded man was pulled forward into the position of a religious submissive. 'You bastard,' he croaked dismally, blood trickling from his mouth. 'Deacon'll see to y . . . ' His words abruptly tailed off as a massive shudder engulfed his body and then he toppled sideways. As death claimed him, he was still attached to the only piece of furniture in the cell.

It was only then that the enormity of what he had just done struck Lee Madden. He'd just become a premeditated killer and the thought didn't sit well. Then again, having lost his only brother, he recognized that there would likely be more blood spilt before justice was done. And he didn't get any opportunity to ponder over it either. Without warning, the guardhouse door opened with a thump.

Into the room tramped Lieutenant Fleming and one enlisted man. Apparently it was time to change the guard and they couldn't have chosen a worse time. Taken completely by surprise, the

155

officer stumbled over the unconscious sentry and only just avoided a fall. That brief setback allowed Lee the time to react. Having no further use for the bow and arrows, he hurled them at the two bluecoats and followed that up by drawing and cocking his revolver.

'Keep that flap holster fastened, Lieutenant, and nobody will get hurt,' Lee commanded.

Fleming peered around the room in horrified disbelief, his eyes lingering longest on the civilian's bloodied corpse. 'This night's work has guaranteed you the hang man, Madden,' he announced heatedly.

Lee shook his head emphatically. 'Well I don't see it that way. Your men are just sleeping it off and that low-life deserved to die. An eye for an eye, as the Bible says. So now the two of you are going to drag this soldier boy over to that cell and lock yourselves in with the drunk fella.'

The lieutenant squared his shoulders and glared back. 'I don't think so. You said you were in the army yourself once. So I don't reckon you'd gun us both down in cold blood.'

Lee's eyes narrowed dangerously as the muzzle of his revolver settled unwaveringly on the officer's chest. 'Are you ready to bet your life on that, mister?'

For a brief moment Fleming held his gaze. Then his eyes flicked on to the gory cadaver and suddenly his shoulders sagged.

'C'mon, sir,' said the enlisted man softly. 'We'll get another chance at him. Just see if we don't.'

Together the two men heaved the unconscious sentry over to the cell and allowed Lee to lock them in. 'Sorry it had to end this way, fellas,' he remarked as he headed for the door.

'It ain't ended . . . yet,' came Fleming's angry response and then their jailer was out into the night, throwing the keys off under the nearest boarding.

9

Martha Chandler didn't care to admit it, but she was worried about what the future held. After three days' hard slog, Fort Laramie seemed like a distant memory. And yet according to the only man amongst them who had ever covered the ground before, everything was only going to get harder.

The trail would continue to parallel the North Platte for the next 180 miles or so, until that river took a steep dive southwards just before Independence Rock. From there the route continued west past the gorge known as Devil's Gate, only it would then be following the Sweetwater River all the way to South Pass, the lowest point through the Rocky Mountains.

Apart from the Mormon 'oasis' at Salt Lake City, there would be no further contact with any form of civilization until they finally reached Oregon Territory. For now, the settlers had an uphill grind through the foothills of the Rockies. Their endurance and determination would be tested as never before. Lush grass had given way to sage and greasewood and there was no longer a distinct path.

Because of the conditions, Martha and the children now had to guide and cajole their team of oxen up the tricky gradients just to maintain a steady progress. As the reality of what actually lay ahead dawned on her, the young widow began to fear for her family's prospects. If she hadn't completely acknowledged one particular fact before, she certainly did now. Even with plucky youngsters, a woman couldn't hope to cope without a man and Lee Madden hadn't been seen since that last night at the fort.

Two days after their departure, a patrol of mounted soldiers had swooped down on the column with obvious intentions. All the settlers had heard about the brutal murder in the guardhouse and it appeared that Madden was now a wanted man twice over. They mostly believed that the dead thug had deserved his fate and had truthfully answered the army's questions. They had no idea of the fugitive's whereabouts and didn't especially care. But that wasn't true of Martha. She realized that she cared a lot and not all of it was self-serving,

'You look like you've lost a dollar and found a peso,' quipped William Bent, a short while after the bluecoats had moved on. He had unexpectedly appeared at her side and read much from her distracted expression. 'You'll need to keep more alert than that. Whether he rejoins us or not, we've got our first big test coming up soon.'

Martha didn't like the strange gleam in his eye. It was as though the old mountain man had seen into her soul. Yet since he obviously had more to say, she chose to remain silent.

'Up yonder a piece there's a ridge.

160

It's mucho steep and there's no way around it without wasting precious days in a detour. So we have to go straight up it. It's going to need ropes and a lot of muscle . . . both man and beast to heave all these wagons up.'

She knew then that he was coming to the cruncher.

Bent at least had the good grace to appear uncomfortable. 'Thing is, there's been a lot of talk by the others that you're slowing them down and they do have a point.' He paused to noisily clear his throat. 'There's no easy way to say this. So here goes. You're not in the lead any more. In fact you're the new back marker.'

A fire came into her belly that took both him and her by surprise. 'Just like that, eh? Well that's just dandy,' she snarled. 'My husband gets killed by heathen savages and all of a sudden none of the men want to know me . . . at least not with their wives in tow. This wouldn't be happening if Lee was here and you

161

know it. They wouldn't have the guts!'

Bent stared at her for a moment and then smiled sadly. 'No, you're right. They wouldn't. But the fact is, he isn't here and it is happening. And I'll tell you this. I wish he was here, because I don't think we've seen the last of that border trash. There might only be five of them left, but they could give us an awful lot of trouble if they caught us unawares.'

★   ★   ★

The massive war party was of sufficient size to have easily overwhelmed the five white men in a surprise attack, regardless of their weaponry. Horses, guns and all possessions would have been theirs for the taking. The band of Oglala Sioux had swept in from Nebraska Territory some days earlier in search of plunder and scalps. Whether these came from their traditional tribal enemies or from the steadily encroaching *Wasi'chu* mattered little to them. From the very first encounter of the Sioux tribes with the Lewis and Clark expedition half a century earlier, the Indians' hostility had been clearly demonstrated. And yet, the behaviour of these particular white men was sufficiently intriguing for the war chief to hold his impatient warriors in check.

Eagle Foot lay on his belly, basking in the warm sunshine. He had removed his ornate war bonnet and was carefully scrutinizing the five men down below. They had taken pains to conceal their horses well out of earshot and were plainly waiting for someone or something. Positioned behind large boulders, just above and well to the side of the summit of a very steep incline, they were passing the time by meticulously cleaning their firearms. The chief absorbed all this and came to a decision. The interlopers were obviously intending to have to fight for something of importance. Possibly many animals or weapons or maybe even some 'fire water'. Many of the warriors had developed an unquenchable taste for that potent liquid, which was very difficult to forgo.

So when the outcome of any conflict had been decided, the Sioux would move in and claim everything remaining for themselves. Eagle Foot could then rightly claim the kudos due to a cunning and successful war chief. All he had to do in the meantime was keep the leash on his restless braves.

⋆   ⋆   ⋆

'I tells you there's someone or something watching us. I can feel it in my water,' Brady asserted stubbornly.

'So go take a piss,' Swain snapped back. 'That way you won't feel it any more!' With that, he returned to his task of running an oily cloth through the barrel of his Sharps rifle. If he noticed Brady staring morosely at him, then he chose not to show it. The man was an addle-brained oaf and he had more important things on his mind. The loss, to a federal jail, of another of his gang irked him considerably and yet there was little he could do about it. An army post was just too tough a nut even for him to crack. And then there was Lee Madden. What if he hadn't rejoined the wagon train at all and was instead maybe laying out on the plains somewhere with a barbed arrow in his guts? Such an unsatisfactory end to their murderous quest would be just too much of a disappointment. He and his men would simply have to take their frustrations out on the damn fool settlers. At least then they could return to Kansas as rich men.

★ ★ ★

'So now's the time to dump all that furniture you just had to bring along,' William Bent laconically remarked. He knew full well that the more testing stretches of the Oregon Trail were littered with discarded possessions. He and Jake had graphically warned everyone about this likely outcome back in Independence, but only now did they appreciate its true significance.

The settlers were congregated at the foot of a frighteningly steep incline. It was to be their first real test of teamwork and many of them were worried. Yet Bent wasn't inclined to go easy on them. Ideally, he wanted them angry at the situation and fired up for the challenge.

'Getting to the top will require plenty of good rope and more sweat than you can imagine, so all you want to be keeping in those wagons is necessities. Food and supplies for the journey and seeds for planting in Oregon.' His eyes locked briefly with Martha's and he favoured her with a sympathetic smile. It occurred to him that Lee Madden could have chosen a better time to turn assassin, but then it was back to business. 'I'm going to check out the summit, while you folks get organized.

If you can't decide who's going first, try drawing straws. Ha ha!'

With that, he turned away and urged his mount up the hill. Even on a willing horse with a light load, it took the scout quite some time to get to the top. In addition to the steep gradient, the going was uneven with many large stones creating a hazard. Finally he reached the top and gratefully dismounted to view his surroundings. It was much as he remembered. As though by way of reward for the effort expended, the ground levelled out like a plateau for a mile or two before continuing its relentless climb to the Rockies. Within spitting distance, there were a number of smooth boulders ideally placed to assist in hauling the wagons up.

Cupping his hands, Bent bellowed down, 'Let's get moving, folks. Get some beasts up here and plenty of rope.'

★　★　★

Martha felt a strange emptiness inside as she watched the explosion of activity along the wagon train from her new position at its rear. It was the emptiness of exclusion. Nobody had said as much, but it was obvious that she was to remain at the back. Only when everyone else had reached the summit was she likely to get her chance and even then only if Bent ordered it or some of those men with kinder hearts offered to help. As an attractive lone female, she was both an encumbrance and a threat. Not for the first time that day, Martha fervently wished that Lee would rejoin her and set matters aright.

It was because of her inactivity that she was the first to notice that trouble was brewing. With William Bent temporarily out of the picture, impotent anger at the necessary load-lightening measures was showing itself amongst some of the men. Jugs of whiskey obtained in Fort Laramie at extortionate prices began to appear and the mood soon turned ugly. Ignoring their wives' demands for restraint, a group of men led by Rufus Barlow began to rail at the apparent injustice. Taking great swigs at the harsh liquid, they started to come up with all kinds of unreasonable suggestions.

'If we doubled up the teams on each wagon, we could still get all our furniture up that goddamned hill!'

'That old bastard up there don't care, 'cause he ain't got a thing to his name anyhu!'

'I say we do it our way and to hell with him. He's gone the way of the beaver . . . all trapped out!'

'Why not triple team them? If he don't like it, we just ram one of these jugs up his ass. That'll show him.'

And so it went on . . .

★   ★   ★

Always reliable, Ethan Wells and his family were to be the first to join the grizzled scout on the plateau. Thad, now fully recovered, had slowly driven their oxen before him up the punishingly steep slope, all the while unfurling two thick cables of rope, which were securely fastened to the front axle of his parent's wagon. He found Bent to be strangely subdued and the boy's unwelcome news only added to his dark expression.

'Some of those fellas are hitting the joy juice mighty hard down there, Mr Bent,' remarked Thad, in a pretty fair attempt at maturity. 'My pa reckons that the prospect of dumping so many of their possibles didn't appeal.'

'Goddamn it all,' Bent exclaimed angrily. 'If they'd done listened to me in the first place, they wouldn't be in this fix! Their loss will be other people's gain and it's not like they've got money to burn . . . or time to waste getting drunk.'

He well knew that some enterprising frontier trading outfits actually sent wagons out on to the most frequented trails to recover cast-off items and sell them back east. The fact that they had probably sold the objects to the settlers in the first place was an added sweetener. Grinding his teeth, the former mountain man furiously scratched at his chin with a set of grubby fingers. Bearing sole responsibility for the large wagon train was beginning to gnaw at him and the prospect of exchanging it for a solitary life in the mountains was suddenly very appealing. And yet, there could be no quitting because he had given his word to Jake Twelvetrees and his generation actually kept their promises, however grudgingly given. Suddenly coming to a decision, he pointed at a huge smooth boulder. The marks of previous expeditions plainly showed.

'I reckon that'll answer. Take a turn round it with those cables and get your wagon up here, pronto.' His expression suddenly softened and he favoured the boy with an encouraging smile. 'I might as well wait up here for a while longer. That way I can tell your ma and pa just how well you're handling all this responsibility.'

Thad beamed with delight and then waved down to signal his parents. Yet as Bent turned away, all animation drained out of his features. Taking a firm grip of his rifle, he carefully scanned the surrounding area. After decades in the wilderness, the former mountain man could sense danger and yet he couldn't stop the whole wagon train on just a hunch.

Even with the massive rock acting as a pulley, the amount of effort required to bring the wagon up was immense. Ethan and Rose had listened to advice and sensibly not over-burdened it, but even so it took a great deal of urging by Thad to keep the oxen straining across the flat land. With his parents heaving on the wheels, the unmanned wagon gradually inched its way up the steep slope until at last it arrived undamaged at the summit. Its owners thankfully collapsed on the level ground and drew in great gulps of air. Sweat poured from their faces and their clothes were sodden.

Leaving them to rest, Bent took a hammer from under the bench seat and used it to free off the great cables around the axle. He too was panting by the time he had tugged them loose. Yet despite the exercise and the positive start to the operation, Bent remained unsettled.

Hauling on the rope ends, he approached the two relieved settlers and softly announced, 'Keep your long gun to hand and your eyes peeled, Ethan. I've got a nose for trouble and something just doesn't smell right up here. If it wasn't for those damn fools getting liquored up, I'd send your Thad back down with the ropes. As it is I've got to go and crack a few heads.' With that he took a last lingering look at the surrounding hills and then set off back to the wagon train.

Unnerved by the scout's warning, Ethan suddenly felt very exposed up on the plateau. The comparison between his situation and that of when the Chandlers' lone wagon waited beyond the South Platte crossing point was not lost on him. Abruptly aware that his wife and son were staring anxiously at him, he forced a smile and then vigorously slapped his hands together. 'Unfurl those cables, Thad,' he ordered. 'Mr Bent needs the slack to get the next wagon up.' As he lifted his rifle out of the wagon bed, he knew that that occurrence couldn't come too soon for him.

* * *

'Let's take 'em now, Deacon. While that old buzzard's out of the way.' James Sweet was about the only member of Swain's reduced gang who possessed half a brain, but his leader wasn't interested in such entreaties. He was too busy running his spyglass up and down the stationary column of wagons.

'Hush up Jim. I'm still looking for that murdering cuss, Madden. And besides, I want a few more of them up here first, to make it worth our while.'

Brady, who normally struggled to cope with any consecutive thoughts, was strangely quiet. Fingering his revolver, he continued to glance uneasily up at the hills behind him. What he lacked in intelligence was to some extent made up for by raw animal instinct and he could almost taste trouble. Finally, he could remain silent no longer. 'For Christ's sake. There's something up in those rocks, Deacon. I want to take me a look around. It can't do any harm while you're just laying there.' That last bit was said in a whine that was guaranteed to irk his boss.

Aggressively twisting around, Swain snarled through gritted teeth, 'So do it, but keep your fool head down. If you show yourself to those pilgrims down there, I'll damn well shoot you myself!' With that, he turned back to his obsessive scrutiny and barely even noticed as Brady eased carefully away from the group.

Reaching the next wagon in line, William Bent gratefully handed the cables over. Wells' oxen would temporarily take the load again, but more beasts were being chivvied up the incline by wives and children. Rufus and his dissenters were lingering around the rear of the column. They had seen his arrival and were busy imbibing more 'Dutch courage'.

'Keep them moving up that hill, Jacob,' Bent said to the nearest settler. 'Looks like I've got me some vigilantes to take care of!' So saying, he checked the loads of his revolvers before steadily walking down the line. It was unlikely that he would need to resort to gunplay, but strong liquor had a way of changing people's perceptions . . . as he well knew.

As he drew closer, Bent swapped his long rifle over to his left hand and carefully scrutinized the waiting men. As sober individuals, not one of them would have posed a threat, but as a group of rowdy tipplers they obviously considered themselves to be intimidating. Aware of his approach, one of them threw an empty jug at a rock, so that it noisily shattered and they all laughed self-consciously. As he expected, Rufus Barlow had the words. Fired up on 'gut rot', he was preening like a peacock.

'You ain't welcome here, mountain man,' he proclaimed with slurred pretension. 'Nobody tells us what to keep and what to throw away. We'll double or even triple team the wagons if necess . . . if necessi . . . if needs be.' With that, he moved forward until he was mere inches away and proceeded to jab his right forefinger into Bent's buckskin-clad chest. 'So you just keep your nose out of our business and stick to trailing runaways . . . or whatever it is you do.' Those around him guffawed at his alcohol-fuelled insolence.

Without any warning, Bent's right hand moved with the speed of a striking snake, but remarkably it didn't contain a weapon. Seizing hold of Rufus's outstretched finger, he viciously snapped it back. The sharp

crack was heard by all his drunken supporters, as was the howl of pain that
followed it. Broken or dislocated, it made
no difference because the result was the
same. Overcome with shock, Rufus dropped
down on to his knees in front of the
scout as though in supplication. As the
pathetic figure begged for release, the barrel of the Hawken rifle rose and then
fell sharply on to his defenceless skull.
The blow was sufficient to stun the suddenly clear-headed settler without actually
rendering him unconscious.

Having turned the tables with chilling ease, William Bent regarded the
cowed spectators with thinly veiled
malevolence. Not one of them had
shown any inclination to intervene and
now they merely stood and awaited his
next words.

'Any of you sorry-looking sons of
bitches ever prods me in the chest
again, you'll lose the finger. I might be a
bit long in the tooth, but I've seen and
done things you pus weasels couldn't
even dream of. So from now on you'll

walk softly around me. Savvy?'

To a man, they all nodded their agreement.

'Right then. So there'll be no double or triple teaming. We haven't got the time.' There was a momentary hesitation. Christ, he realized, I sound like Twelvetrees!

'Any belongings you can't get up that hill with your own team gets dumped here and now. That little rise is just the start. Them's mountains up ahead and it's only going to get worse. Understand?'

They all nodded dumbly.

'And I don't want to see any more bug juice, 'lessen it's for medicinal purposes.' With that, he pulled the dazed Rufus to his feet. 'C'mon you little snake, snap out of it.'

Hearing movement behind, he twisted around, poised to counter another threat. To his surprise he saw Martha Chandler weaving her way through the dispersing men. With a set expression on her face, she walked up to the two of them. Drawing back her right hand to its fullest extent, she landed a tremendous slap right across Rufus's left cheek, leaving a bright red weal mark.

'My daughter didn't run away, Rufus Barlow. She was stolen from me and this man helped get her back. Him and Lee Madden both . . . wherever the hell he might be!'

With that, she turned away leaving Bent bemused and Barlow reeling. Such was their preoccupation that the single gunshot up on the hill took everybody by surprise.

10

'The hell with this,' snarled Deacon Swain bitterly. 'If that tarnal cockchafer is down there, then it's as a shape shifter!'

Roughly contracting his drawtube spyglass, he backed away from the cluster of rocks on his hands and knees. Three of his men were expectantly awaiting orders.

'Where the hell's Brady?' he demanded angrily.

'He went off looking for ghosts, remember?' responded Sweet in a manner that suggested he really couldn't care less.

'Jesus H. Christ!' Swain responded heatedly. 'If we lose any more, we'll be reduced to begging for dimes.'

Drawing in a deep breath, the gang leader briefly pondered their situation before coming to a hurried decision.

Lee Madden's trail had obviously gone cold and he'd had a belly full of wandering around the great American wilderness. It was time to snatch some easy pickings and head back east. If he'd been in a more contemplative frame of mind, he might have given some serious thought to Brady's strange disappearance, but sadly it was not to be.

'Right, listen up. There's two wagons for the taking and another on its way up. We'll strip them of everything worth cash money and then get the hell out of here.' Nodding to one of the men, he ordered, 'Break out those swords. It's time to put the fear of God into those pilgrims.'

★ ★ ★

Scant minutes later, the four men appeared on the diminutive plateau and raced towards the startled settlers. Ethan Wells had done as instructed. He had his rifle at the ready, but was also out in the open observing the progress of the third wagon. He should have leapt for the nearest cover but, going by instinct rather than good sense, instead levelled his gun at the closest rider and took hurried aim. Then, as the horses thundered closer, raw fear overcame resolve and his left arm began to tremble uncontrollably. Try as he might, Ethan just couldn't get the muzzle to settle on flesh and blood. And then it was simply too late.

Deacon Swain had been born to a life of raiding and rapine. To him, killing other human beings was second nature. Keeping low in the saddle, he calmly lined his Colt up on the wavering figure and fired. Even as his weapon discharged, he veered sharply off to his left towards the wagons. He had no doubt at all that he had put his man down.

The ball struck Wells high in his left shoulder, breaking the collarbone and in the process quite literally knocked him off his feet. Following him down, the heavy barrel of his own rifle then struck the luckless settler on his forehead, leaving him stunned and temporarily anaesthetized.

'Ethan!' his wife screamed out in abject horror. Then her attention was taken by the men surrounding her wagon.

'We want everything you've got of value,' Swain demanded. 'If I have to ask twice, we'll torch your wagon.' Gesturing at the other one, he added, 'Jim, check it out, while I see what's occurring down below.'

Sweet did as instructed, his revolver cocked and ready. That family, going by the name of Ketchum, had witnessed Wells' fate and put up no resistance. Instead they grabbed all the coins and trinkets that they could find and held them out to him. By way of encouragement, the seasoned marauder holstered his gun and then lashed out at the wagon's canvas cover with his broadsword. As great rents appeared in the material, one of the two children screamed out in terror. 'Give him everything, Pa. Just make him go away!'

Swain gazed down the steep slope to see how the main body of settlers were reacting to his men's sudden arrival. A third wagon had reached about halfway, but was now static, as Thad Wells had abruptly ceased driving the oxen. All those accompanying it were milling around in confusion. The gun thug considered adding to that by slashing through the cables, but then thought better of it. Another wagon would mean more pickings.

'Get those animals moving, son,' he yelled at Thad. 'Or you'll be the worse for it.'

The lad had already turned his back on the oxen and was heading for his stricken father. 'You can go to hell, mister,' he cried out gamely. 'You've just shot my pa!'

Not even his own kin talked to Deacon Swain like that. Swiftly aiming his revolver, he barked back, 'You've got grit, boy, I'll give you that. But don't dare provoke me. I ain't never busted a cap on a child before, but I might just give it a try this day!'

Thad's fresh-faced features registered real fear. The memory of his shooting accident was still raw and he wasn't about to risk incurring a second wound. Reluctantly he turned around and returned to the beasts, leaving his father sprawled on the ground.

★   ★   ★

'What do we do, Mr Bent?' demanded a white-faced settler. Rufus Barlow's minor injury was abruptly irrelevant and all traces of belligerence had left the men, because they quite simply had no one else to turn to.

That man glanced up at the plateau. He noticed that Swain had wisely backed away from the edge. The stranded wagon had slowly begun to move up the hill again, but all the people were hurrying back down.

186

'I ain't got any kind of a shot.' Patting the barrel of his Hawken, he added, 'Even with this beauty, I need to be able to see the target. But there can't be many of them up there, so if any of you good people want to join me, we could always rush them.'

As he had expected, there were no takers.

'That's what I figured,' he responded sarcastically. 'In that case, you'd better circle the wagons, just in case they take it into their heads to mosey on down here.'

The overlanders didn't need any second prompting. With a frantic burst of activity they had soon formed a defensive ring. It was immediately apparent to William Bent that all they had achieved by such action was a stand-off. Their further progress was stymied, so long as Swain's thugs held the high ground, but all that was about to change.

★   ★   ★

The inhuman scream came from somewhere high up on the hillside. It was long and penetrating and for a brief moment Deacon Swain was completely nonplussed. Even for someone brutalized by years of violence, the sound possessed an eerie, frightening quality. Then, suddenly, realization dawned upon him. Brady had obviously found what he had been looking for and logic dictated that whoever or whatever it was wouldn't stop with him.

'Forget those goddamn toad stabbers,' he bellowed, gesturing with his sword. 'Get your long guns ready.'

The words were barely out of his mouth before there came the thunderous sound of a great many animals on the move. As he watched in awe, a great phalanx of horsemen swept down out of the hills and on to the plateau. They were half-naked and garishly daubed with tribal war paint. Very few of the savages were toting firearms, but with such numbers that mattered little. And what happened next proved beyond all doubt that their intentions were hostile. To a man, they all peered away to their right and so Swain's gaze naturally followed on. Three more figures had appeared on foot, high up in the jumble of rocks. The one in the centre was bathed in blood and firmly gripped by his tormentors.

Brady had inflicted great suffering on many anti-slavery supporters, but now it was most definitely his turn. The gun thug's scalp had already been cleanly and agonizingly sliced from his head and as his comrades looked on, a razor sharp blade cut deep into his exposed throat. As more blood flowed, his captors suddenly hurled him forward on to the waiting rocks like so much discarded rubbish. The assembled warriors howled out their jubilant appreciation, before turning their attention to the horrified whites.

'Sweet Jesus,' yelled one of the Kansas roughnecks. 'We're up shit creek now!'

Swain's earlier threat now counted

for little and Thad raced back to his parent's wagon to rejoin his mother and sister. None of the remaining marauders even thought to stop him and without his exhortations, the third wagon came to a halt some way below the crest. The other settlers abandoned their own conveyance and rushed to link up with the three of them. Then together they all streamed over to the top of the steep slope. In their path lay Ethan Wells, who was only now beginning to come round.

★　★　★

From his position at the centre of his men, Eagle Foot glanced from side to side. A fresh bloody trophy hung from his lance. It was his intention that there would soon be many more of them. His men had travelled far in search of scalps and plunder and now they were to get their just reward. He nodded and the massed warriors uttered a collective howl before urging their horses into a walk. The noise and slow pace was deliberate, designed to unnerve their enemies and in this particular instance, the tactic served them well.

★ ★ ★

'The hell with this,' yelled Swain to his men. His next course of action had suddenly become blindingly obvious. 'The only place for us is in amongst those pilgrims. Let's ride!'

With all thoughts of thievery forgotten, the four of them galloped for the crest. They reached it at the same time as the fleeing settlers. Mingling with them meant that the Kansas raiders were safe from retribution from below, but time was running out on the plateau. Thad and his mother, Rose, were desperately attempting to get Ethan on to his feet, but even together they lacked the brute strength needed to lift a helpless full-grown man. Blood coated his torso and each movement brought forth pitiful cries of pain. It

191

suddenly dawned on her that if, as appeared likely, his collarbone was smashed, then they had no chance of moving him without a wagon.

Behind them, the Indians had dramatically stepped up the pace and any semblance of order had gone. Whooping and hollering they raced across the plateau, intent on lifting more scalps. Swain and his men unleashed a ragged volley at the fast-moving aggressors and one horse went down, but the rest of them just kept on coming. The occupants of the second wagon were already bounding down the slope, crying out a warning to those below.

⋆ ⋆ ⋆

William Bent and the settlers could only wonder at the cause of all this mayhem. They had all heard Brady's chilling howl of agony, but nobody had actually seen anything since then. What was apparent though, was that Swain's thugs were no longer the prime assailants.

'Roll one of those wagons back,' the scout instructed. 'We need to get those folks under cover fast.'

★   ★   ★

Swain motioned for his men to follow him down the steep slope, ignoring Thad and his mother as they frantically struggled with Ethan. The devil take them, he decided.

'Don't leave us!' Rose pleaded. The torment and anguish on her face was plain to see. 'If they take Ethan he'll be tortured for sure.'

Deacon Swain was nothing if not ruthless, but he was also a realist. In a flash, he recognized the benefit of arriving at the wagon train with rescued settlers, but also understood that Ethan was a lost cause. Glancing over at Sweet he commanded, 'Get the woman down there . . . alive.' Then he leaned out of the saddle and grabbed Thad by his collar. With an impressive display of animal strength, he heaved the boy up over the saddle horn and then pointed his revolver directly at Ethan's head.

Even as the son cried out, 'No!' he squeezed the trigger and brutally snuffed out the father's life.

At that moment an arrow flashed past his own head. It travelled so close that he actually felt the fletching score his skin. It was definitely time to leave. With Thad crying and struggling on his lap, Swain urged his mount down the incline, all the while praying that whoever was in charge down there had the sense to provide some covering fire.

★   ★   ★

Martha Chandler watched in horror as the gang leader calmly murdered Ethan Wells. So now there was another widow in the wagon train. She wondered just how many more there would be by the time they reached Oregon . . . if any of them ever did.

The mishmash of outlaws and settlers were about halfway down the hill when the first of the Indians reached the crest. At the sight of the defensive circle they halted in confusion and waited for some sign from their leader. William Bent was in no doubt about what needed to be done. 'That's a goddamn Sioux war party up there. Pile it in to them!'

So saying, he took careful aim down the long barrel of his Hawken and squeezed the trigger. With an encouraging roar, the old gun discharged. The heavy ball knocked a warrior backwards off his mount and succeeded in breaking the spell of horrified inaction that had gripped the settlers at the first sight of the hostiles. Suddenly galvanized into activity, they clustered between the wagons and fired a ragged volley up the slope. Hastily executed it did little damage, but served notice that they were at least prepared to fight.

With the Indians temporarily halted, the refugees from the plateau were able to make it to the dubious safety of the wagon train. Those on foot gratefully rushed through the prepared gap, closely followed by Swain and his men.

'Fill that breach,' Bent commanded as he quickly reloaded his rifle. He was well aware that his next target might well be a white man.

As the horsemen came to a halt in the transient compound, Thad and his mother both hastily fled from their 'saviours'. 'That pig killed my pa,' the boy proclaimed loudly, the second his feet touched the ground.

Swain regarded him through narrowed eyes. 'That's a mite ungrateful, sonny,' he remarked softly. 'Seems to me I was just saving him from a slow and painful death. Him being disabled an' all.'

That was just too much for Rose Wells. Her normally placid features turned scarlet as she screamed out accusingly, 'It was you done shot him in the first place, you cowardly bastard!'

The gang leader peered calmly

around him. Many of the settlers were staring at him with sullen hostility and he was conscious that all the escape routes were sealed off against the Indians' next move. The only remaining course of action was for he and his men to tough it out, which was something that he happened to be good at. With a cold smile, he slowly dismounted and stood ready, his right hand hovering close to one of Colonel Colt's revolvers. 'So what happens next?' he enquired evenly.

It was then that he noticed William Bent for the first time. The tall, rangy, white-haired scout stepped away from the assembled settlers, his rifle cocked and ready. He had the look of a man who had been everywhere and done everything. His grizzled features were hard and uncompromising.

'The man with the Hawken,' Swain acknowledged coolly. 'I wondered if we'd ever bump into you.'

Bent surveyed him like he might an insect that he was about to crush.

Wordlessly he moved forward, closing the distance steadily but unhurriedly. He could sense Swain's momentary indecision as that man pondered a suitable response. If the gun thug was going to draw a weapon, then he needed to do it while there was still room for manoeuvre, yet such a hostile action didn't fit well with claiming sanctuary from the Sioux war party. And then abruptly the two men were almost nose-to-nose and it was too late for any gunplay.

'So you'll be Deacon Swain, huh?' Bent observed conversationally as he slammed the butt of his rifle in hard. It caught the other man in his belly and drew a sharp grunt of pain, but remarkably he stayed on his feet. Slowly straightening up again, Swain glanced quickly at his three men and shook his head. Just like his assailant, he well knew that a gunfight at that particular time would only benefit the savages massing on the plateau.

'That was a payment on account for

Jake Twelvetrees,' Bent continued, before hammering in another even harder blow. 'And that was for Ethan Wells, who never hurt anyone in his life as far as I know.'

This time Swain doubled over, retching and groaning from the pain that spread throughout his midriff. It was some time before he was able to raise his head and all the time the sound of chanting came from the plateau. It was as though the Sioux were holding off until the contest below them had been decided.

'You've got some real hard bark on you, mister,' Swain finally managed.

Bent remained close, ready to use his rifle as a club again if necessary. 'You take shit off a man, he'll just give you more shit. That's something these good folks don't seem to have learned yet.'

With a concerted effort, Swain carefully drew himself erect. 'Fine words. I'll ponder them while we deal with those foolish savages up there.' There could be no mistaking the menace in what followed. 'Then we'll have a reckoning, before one of us goes on his way.'

Before Bent had any chance of offering a response, the noise above grew to a frightening crescendo and then one of the settlers bellowed out, 'Take cover. They're fixing to fire.'

With the compelling confrontation temporarily forgotten, everyone rushed for concealment behind a wagon. They were only just in time, as a ragged volley of musketry crashed out and flying lead slammed into the timbers.

'What do you think they'll do next, Mr Bent?'

That man glanced round to find Martha Chandler crouching anxiously beside him. He sighed regretfully before answering. 'That's for us to find out. Meantime you'd do best comforting Rose Wells. You more than anyone knows what it's like to lose a husband.'

Without awaiting any reply, he moved off swiftly and fetched up in the middle of the Kansas thugs as they crouched behind a wagon bed. Fixing his eyes steadily on their leader he stated, 'If any of us are to survive this, we'll have to work together. Yes?'

Swain nodded cautiously and Bent continued. 'My guess is they'll cut loose that wagon on the hillside and then follow it in from any which way. If we try to shift the wagons to avoid it, it'll mean breaking up the circle and those sons of bitches'll catch us on the move and cut us to pieces.'

James Sweet was nervous and on edge. 'You sure are all shit and no sugar. So just what are we supposed to do, mountain man?'

Bent completely ignored him and continued to stare at Deacon Swain. 'I reckon you fellas are used to killing and I know I am. So wherever that wagon hits, is where we need to be. So long as we don't scare, we've got a chance.'

The gang leader returned his stare for a long moment before, quite amazingly, the faintest hint of a smile crossed his brutal features. 'One question?'

Engrossed in their Indian problem, Bent viewed him expectantly.

'Where the hell is Lee Madden? Because he's the only reason we're in this goddamn mess.'

Taken slightly aback, the scout chuckled. 'He had business in Fort Laramie with the one you left behind. I believe it led to bloodshed.'

It was Swain's turn to be surprised. 'He actually went after one of my men in an army stockade. Son of a bitch!'

11

It was the sight of the conveniently stranded wagon that made up his mind. Like most Indians, Eagle Foot was heavily influenced by spirits and omens. That the white eyes should provide an instrument for their own destruction was most definitely a good omen and one to be seized on. Yet careful timing was needed, because the gradient was just too steep to chance a combined headlong rush.

Barking out orders, he sent the main body of his warriors off along the crest to descend out of range of the settlers' rifles. After chewing on some pemmican to pass the time, Eagle Foot dismounted near the smooth boulder. He drew his hunting knife and began to saw on the thick cables. The team of oxen were munching on the sparse grass some distance away, their inertia keeping the wagon in place. Once freed, they would be driven off by their new owners to be butchered for food.

With the weakening ropes creaking under the strain, the war chief dropped on to all fours and crawled over to the edge. His men were in position. It was time to strike. He screamed out, down the hill, 'Hookahey! Hookahey! Hopo!

Those words echoed back to him as all the warriors took up the cry. As instructed, they dug their heels in to their ponies' flanks and launched themselves at the wagon train. With savage delight, Eagle Foot twisted back to the ropes and viciously slashed at them. Within seconds they parted and the wagon suddenly became an unstoppable weapon of extreme power.

* * *

'They're on the move!'

'My God, so's our wagon,' wailed one of the survivors from the hillside. Emitting tremendous rattling and creaking sounds, it rolled relentlessly towards its owners, the iron-shod wheels picking up speed at a terrifying rate the nearer it got. Those settlers directly in its path fled for their lives, but not so William Bent and his unsavoury new allies from Kansas. They remained close, trying to gauge the deadly projectile's exact point of impact. Beyond the circle, the thundering of hooves also drew nearer and the scattered men folk began to get twitchy.

'Hold your fire until you can smell them,' the scout bellowed. He well knew that no rifle was accurate to any kind of range in nervous hands.

The agonizing wait was soon over. With explosive force, the runaway wagon piled into its static counterpart, catching it at the rear. There was a tremendous splintering crash, which could be heard far beyond the immediate area. Its combined weight and momentum was sufficient to ram the other vehicle sideways. As pots and pans and other possessions cascaded over the waiting men, the defensive circle was effectively ruptured. Together, the two wagons continued to perform an ungainly pirouette back into the compound. It was only as the edges of their buckled wheels dug into the hard ground that they finally came to a grinding halt.

The favoured Indian tactic when attacking a circled wagon train was to gallop around it, firing into the defenders and tightening the noose ready for a final rush. Not so this time. Following Eagle Foot's orders, the Sioux war party charged directly for the breach, all the time howling like banshees.

'Let 'em have it,' Bent yelled at the overlanders, as he and the Kansas ruffians rushed forward to board the wrecked wagons. Clambering into the chaotic interiors, the five men levelled their weapons. Only by rapid close quarter firing would they have any chance of repelling the aggressors. Deacon Swain winked broadly at the mountain man.

'Noisy sons of bitches, ain't they?'

A volley of rifle fire rippled out around part of the circle. As a cloud of sulphurous smoke enveloped the wagons, those settlers that owned revolvers quickly discarded their long guns and drew them. In such a fight, even modern breechloaders like the Sharps rifle were just too slow to reload. Those women to hand grabbed them and levered down the falling blocks prior to inserting a new paper cartridge. If they knew their business, they would also have thought ahead and stuffed a handful of percussion caps in their pockets.

The seasoned gunhands defending the gap had each managed to account for one of the enemy, but even as the riderless ponies raced into the compound, more Indians pressed in through the narrow space. Gripping the Hawken's smoking barrel, Bent swung at the nearest warrior. With a resounding thump, the butt smashed into his cheekbone, sending him reeling down to the hard earth. Dropping the rifle like a hot coal, the scout drew a revolver and began firing into the seedling mass. With Swain and his men joining in, the gunfire became an incessant din, but they were all aware that they could only maintain such a rate of fire for a limited time. Once emptied, the weapons were an absolute bitch to reload, even with spare pre-charged cylinders.

Emboldened by the presence of five fierce fighting men, the settlers moved in closer to the conflict and blasted the Sioux with hot lead from all sides. The level of noise and violence was almost indescribable and in such circumstances the Indians' tactics began to count against them. They were concentrated on a narrow front and so could not use their superior speed and manoeuvrability. Faced with such a withering fire, they were unable to break through and soon despair began to set in. With their war chief missing at the crucial moment, the warriors' advance began to stall.

Yet the defenders were both taking casualties and rapidly running out of charged weapons. For a few moments it was touch and go, but then abruptly the Sioux turned tail and careered away. If they had been more perceptive, they might have realized that they were no longer under fire, but they were just too desperate to get clear of the killing ground. For their part, the white men had literally discharged all their guns and so were temporarily almost defenceless. It had been a damned close run thing and William Bent knew it.

'Get your backs against this wreck and plug the gap,' he roared at anyone who would listen.

With their faces blackened by powder residue, the settlers just stared at him in stunned silence. They appeared bewildered at their victory and yet there was just too much to do for them to be allowed any breathing space. And too little time to do it in!

'You don't mean that they'll be back?' queried a man named Ketchum.

'After all that killing.' He and his family had narrowly escaped the plateau and couldn't believe that such slaughter could continue.

Even though most of them were deeply affected by the pitiful moaning of the wounded, all eyes, including those of Swain and his men, were on Bent. He was the only one with experience of fighting Indians and he possessed an undeniable aura of assurance and authority. 'Damn right they'll be back,' that man retorted. 'At least for one more charge. Their chief wasn't with them the first time round. He'll be out there now, cajoling and arguing. So I'll say it one more time. Get your backs against these timbers. We've got to block off this opening and keep them outside the circle. And I want all you women tending to the wounded and reloading anything that'll shoot!' He turned to Deacon Swain and lowered his voice. 'I'd take it kindly if you'd check on the Sioux fallen,' he remarked pointedly. 'There's no way we can watch over prisoners and those varmints have a way of playing possum that would catch us off guard. I reckon you'll be a mite less squeamish than these other folks.'

Swain snorted loudly, but nevertheless did as requested. Drawing their knives, he and his men advanced with chilling purpose on the gunshot Indians sprawled around the compound. Considering how ferocious the encounter had been, it was amazing that only three white men had been wounded. Yet arrow punctures could easily infect and their survival in such circumstances would depend as much on luck as good nursing.

Two of the wagons would never roll again, but with a great deal of exertion the shattered remnants were pushed into place. Bent's sense of terrible urgency, coupled with the grisly killing of the injured Sioux, had infected all the settlers and they feverishly prepared for a second attack. It was well that they did!

Eagle Foot arrived in the midst of his men like a force of nature. Whilst descending from the plateau, his sharp eyes had taken in everything. He well knew that if there was to be a second attack, then it had to take place immediately, before the cursed invaders could reload all their weapons. Whilst his warriors were downcast at their losses, they could not resist his devastating oratory. He would personally lead them in the next and final assault. And this time they would utilize flames as their ally. Detailing half a dozen men to remain behind and create a fire, he bullied and persuaded the others to give it their all for one time more. Again he screamed out, '*Hookahey, Hookahey, Hopo*,' and they all hurtled off towards the beleaguered wagon train, this time with Eagle Foot at their head.

Martha Chandler viewed the returning savages with a deeply heavy heart. She had been helping the other wives to reload both rifles and revolvers. It was no easy task, recharging a cap and ball revolver when under great strain. Each chamber had to be rotated to the correct position, so as to be in line with the weapon's integral ramming lever. It required a measured amount of powder from a flask and then an over-sized lead ball had to be forced in using said rammer. After that a copper percussion cap was placed on the raised nipple. Extreme pressure on that cap, brought on by panic, could result in a detonation that might badly burn the flesh and cause a deadly premature discharge. Even with the task success-fully done, the whole process then had to be repeated five more times.

Seeing the garishly painted Sioux recklessly streaming towards them across the broken ground, she knew that most of the men would only have their single shot rifles ready to meet the threat and the prospect filled her with terror. She gazed around at her equally horrified companions and whispered, 'Is there no one that can save us from these fiends?'

★ ★ ★

Lee Madden had heard the rending crash of the collision before ever he saw anything. He had been shadowing the wagon train for some time, alert for the possible re-appearance of the soldiery from Fort Laramie. It was only when the shooting started that he realized that another, far more baleful force had descended on the settlers. With the North Platte River to his back, he cautiously headed south. As the gunfire reached a crescendo, he decided that there had to be more than just Swain and his border bash involved and so he urged his mount to greater speed. With a full-scale battle going on, his arrival was unlikely to be noticed.

It was just as he neared the crest of a

214

gentle rise that the firing abruptly ceased. Pulling up quickly, Lee ground tethered the reins under a rock and continued on foot. He had feared the worst and yet the sight that awaited him still managed to chill his blood. A huge band of Indians were galloping away from the circled wagons. Some of the animals lacked riders and it was obvious that a deal of blood had been spilt. Then an authority figure arrived from the nearby high ground and order was swiftly restored. After the chief had harangued them for a while, half a dozen figures dismounted and began to construct a fire.

It was clear what was about to happen and Lee was suddenly faced with a momentous decision. He could simply back off and ride away, safe in the knowledge that every hostile in the area seemed to have a prior engagement. Or, he could single-handedly mount an attack that could only be doomed to failure. The choice was obvious, because the settlers had no claim on his loyalty. And yet there was the rub. One of them did. The thought of Martha Chandler ending up as the plaything of some painted buck was just too much to bear. Which meant that he really had no option.

'God dang it all to hell!' he snarled. 'Why did I have to come across someone like her in this wilderness? I should have stayed in Kansas.' That last was a damn lie and he knew it even as he said it.

As the chief urged his warriors forward, Lee scrambled back to his horse and mounted up. He knew that in such appalling circumstances he needed an edge. Surprise would be that edge. The last thing the Indians expected was to be attacked from behind. He would have to ride like the devil and make every ball count.

* * *

'Here they come again,' Bent hollered. His fingers were stained with powder and bleeding from the frantic effort, but he and the Kansas men all had a fully charged rifle and revolver apiece. Not so the settlers, who were far less adept at handling firearms under pressure. Most of them would have to make do with two or three shots at most. 'Dime to a dollar, this'll end up as hand to hand,' he added regretfully. 'And those folks just ain't up to that.'

As Swain cocked the hammer on his Sharps, he replied, 'You handle yourself pretty good, old man. If we survive this, it'll be a real pity to have to kill you, but if you get in my way it'll happen! My oath on that.'

'None of that matters a damn,' Bent scoffed. 'Because if we don't survive, it's the women that I feel sorry for.'

★   ★   ★

The Sioux fire starters glanced up in stunned astonishment, as the big man on a big horse seemed to appear out of nowhere. For a white eye, his riding ability was truly remarkable. He had the reins between his teeth and held a revolver in each hand and yet was in complete control. Amazingly he did not open fire on them, but instead chose to gallop straight through their makings and then continued on after the main body. Howling in anger, they were about to mount up in pursuit, but then recalled Eagle Foot's very explicit instructions. Their chief intended to burn the intruders out and woe betide any of his men that dared to disobey him.

★   ★   ★

Eagle Foot felt a tremendous elation as he pounded towards the circled wagons at the head of his war party. He could feel the muscles of his eager mount working beneath him. Even the need to avoid rocks and indentations could not detract from the joyous experience. Surely nothing could compare to the thrill of warfare. Puffs of smoke burst out as the settlers unleashed a single volley of rifle fire. There were screams around him as a few of his warriors toppled to the ground. Miraculously untouched, he wheeled off to the left so that the circled wagons would remain on his right-hand side. As always, he was confident that the rest of his men would follow. His intention was to keep the white eyes busy until the fire arrows arrived. Then the bloodletting would begin in earnest.

As he and his braves swept around the outer circle loosing arrows as they went, Eagle Foot realized that there was very little return fire. Resuming the offensive immediately had worked. The embattled settlers did not have enough reloaded firearms. A wave of savage joy washed over him as he envisaged the accolades to come. And then something totally unexpected happened. A short distance behind him, there was the distinct crack of a revolver and one of his warriors screamed and slumped forward.

* ★ ★ ★

Lee Madden felt a strange exhilaration settle on him as he overhauled the unsuspecting Sioux. The terrain was dangerously uneven and he was likely to die a bloody death in the next few moments, yet all that only added to the sensation. As he charged along, his heart was beating madly and he actually felt as though he could reach out and touch the nearest warriors. To them, counting coup would have been considered a prestigious act, but sensibly he decided to start killing them instead. Rapidly inserting his horse into the extended column, he took swift aim at the closest broad back and squeezed the trigger. The .36 calibre lead ball punched a satisfyingly bloody hole through flesh and bone and the unsuspecting victim screamed and slumped forward.

The Indians had just commenced their first sweep around the beleaguered settlers and so were completely unprepared to cope with an attack from within their own body. Yet up against such overwhelming numbers, Lee had to strike hard and fast. Urging his horse in between two shrieking savages, he pointed both revolvers at right angles and fired. As the two warriors took mortal wounds and powder burns to their heads, their assailant raised his weapons to the vertical and cocked them. If he should miraculously avoid misfires, there would be nine shots remaining.

Even as his two victims toppled to the ground, Lee was moving on to the next man. With the reins still between his teeth, all control had to be exercised by his legs, but even with the concentration that involved he was still aware of rapturous cheering coming from the wagon circle. As though stung by that, the Oglala in front of him abruptly twisted around to launch a lance strike. Reacting by sheer instinct, Lee wastefully lowered both Colts and fired simultaneously. An evocative cloud of sulphurous smoke swept over him, as his opponent was literally blasted out of the way. That brought him ever closer to his ultimate objective. Lee didn't know Eagle Foot by sight, but recognized him to be the leader and therefore in vital need of slaying. So occupied was he with the multiple demands of remaining mounted, cocking his revolvers and reaching the chief that the lone assassin forgot that he also had enemies behind him.

*   *   *

'Holy shit, that's Lee Madden!' Swain exclaimed incredulously. Instinctively he swung his Sharps over to snap off a shot, but before he got the chance the barrel was roughly forced down.

'You stupid son of a bitch,' bellowed William Bent. 'That man's trying to save all our lives.'

For a highly charged moment, the two men faced each other until finally Swain sighed and the tension temporarily drained from his features. He nodded ruefully, but there was no mistaking the cold menace lurking in his eyes. 'I'll allow you such, but if he survives that lunacy he'll face retribution fro . . . ' An arrow slammed into the wagon bed close to his face and uttering a foul oath, he rapidly aimed his rifle at a fresh target.

★   ★   ★

The war axe sliced through the tender flesh of his back with agonizing precision. Only the fact that Lee had just leaned forward to encourage his horse to greater speed, saved him from a mortal blow. As it was he received a superficial, but very painful wound. Even as blood welled up through his coat, he twisted in the saddle and pointed his right-hand Colt at the axe-wielding Sioux. The warrior's features displayed stark terror as he recognized the inevitability of certain death. Lee squeezed the trigger and was rewarded with a muted pop.

The Indian experienced overwhelming relief, swiftly overlaid by rage, as he again swung his hatchet. Intense pain, horror at the misfire and the necessity to retain his balance all competed with Lee's desperate need to simply stay alive. Ducking low, he again cocked his revolver. The axe head struck the cylinder just as he was taking aim. The jarring blow smashed the gun clean out of his hand. As Lee groaned with shock and frustration, the warrior reversed his grip to try a backhand swing. The grievously pressured white man knew that he only had the one chance left!

Ignoring the tortuous pain in his back, he rapidly twisted around so that his left-hand Colt could be brought to bear. Even as the razor sharp blade again began to seek him out, he squeezed the trigger. With a God-sent crash, the black powder detonated and snuffed out the brave's life in an instant.

With no time to relish his survival, Lee gratefully faced his front. He had now completed a full revolution of the circled wagons. Immediately before him rode the chief in temporary isolation. All the others were pounding along behind the solitary white man and it could surely only be a matter of time before a lucky arrow struck him.

The settlers were managing only a desultory rate of fire and it was obvious that they were having to rely mainly on their single-shot rifles, so he could not hope for much support there. Grabbing the reins in his right hand, he frantically attempted to coax every last bit of speed out of his tiring animal.

Eagle Foot glanced back and was horrified at what he saw. A blood-spattered white man with crazy eyes was manically spurring his horse ever closer. A belt gun that fired many times was being lined up on him. The war chief could not immediately retaliate and so began to frenziedly weave his animal from side to side. Risking another fleeting look, the Sioux was mortified to witness a sort of sick grimace appear on his pursuer's face. Then that man simply lowered his weapon and fired at the far larger target.

The two men just happened to pass directly in front of Martha Chandler's position as the revolver discharged. The leading animal stumbled uncontrollably and hit the ground with brutal force, instantly breaking its neck. The half-naked rider executed a spectacular somersault, witnessed by all his men, and then also landed with pulverizing violence. As Eagle Foot's broken body came to rest, a collective howl of shock and anger rose up from his warriors.

Bizarrely, Lee Madden now found himself at the head of a Sioux war party. He had no idea whether his furious assault had actually achieved anything, but with all the braves in a pack behind him there was no possible benefit to renewing the fight all on his lonesome.

'Get in here, you lunatic,' Martha screamed after him and that suddenly seemed like a very good idea indeed. Brutally reining in his weary animal, he then turned it towards the barricade. At her urging, some of the men dragged barrels and grain sacks from between two wagons and his horse slipped through the temporary gap. Abruptly light-headed and unsteady, he almost fell from the saddle. Strong hands grabbed him and lowered him to the ground.

'You've either got a death wish or a powerful faith in the Lord, Lee Madden!'

He looked up and focused on Martha's lovely powder-smudged features. To his delight, they registered deep concern. She held out a canteen of water and he suddenly realized that his mouth felt like a dry crust. Gratefully slaking his thirst, he impulsively reached out to take her hand. What he was about to say was abruptly halted by a great cry of, 'Fire arrows!' and with a sinking heart he realized that his reckless onslaught had been insufficient at best.

12

'That cockchafer killed my brother and now he's mine!'

Lee's sudden appearance inside the barricades had not gone unnoticed by the Kansas trio. Yet they still didn't have a free hand. As the warning cry hit the settlers like a shock-wave, William Bent remarked, 'You've got some more heathens to kill first, mister!'

The half dozen Oglala Sioux had persevered with their fire starting and were now swiftly approaching with blazing arrows. If any of those flaming projectiles took hold on the sun-dried timbers, the settlers' wagons would be reduced to ashes. In a strangely guttural tongue, the newcomers called out to their comrades for assistance. Although suddenly leaderless, the remaining members of the war party had the sense to realize that a human screen was urgently needed.

The scout bellowed out around the compound, 'Pick those goddamned incendiaries off, or none of you will ever see Oregon!' So saying, he took careful aim with his recharged Hawken. As it crashed out, the large ball ploughed a bloody furrow through one of the six Indians and his flaming arrow descended harmlessly to the barren ground. One down!

'Nice shooting,' Swain grudgingly allowed, as he and his men took aim. 'You must have been quite something, back in the day.'

* * *

At the other side of the enclosure, Martha gasped with alarm at the sight of Lee's blood-soaked back. 'I need to clean that off and bind it up,' she declared firmly. 'Or it's like to infect.'

On the point of acquiescing, he was distracted by the distinctive sound of the big muzzle-loader and glanced over in Bent's direction. The sight of that man's hateful companions momentarily transfixed Lee and drew a snarl of rage from his lips. He couldn't imagine how they came to be fighting side by side, but such considerations were irrelevant. 'There's no time. I have to reload this Navy Six. That piece of shit murdered my brother and he's out to do the same for me.'

Martha recognized his fixed determination and sighed. 'You men just never have enough of killing, do you?' She didn't expect a response and so wasn't disappointed. 'Very well then. Get under this wagon with the children and I'll cover you, but if you disappear on me again, don't even think about coming back!'

As he presented his bloodied back to her and oh so carefully got to his knees, Martha moved with lightning speed. Grabbing a keg of medicinal liquor from under the wagon seat, she uncorked it and liberally poured it over his raw flesh. Howling with pain and indignation, he yelled up at her, 'What the hell did you do that for?'

'You're no good to me rank and putrid,' she blandly replied, before adding mischievously, 'So are you going to load that belt gun or can't you Kansas men hold your drink?'

Muttering incoherent threats, he hastily scrambled under the wagon and came face to face with Marion. The girl gazed at him warmly and then impulsively hugged him. It occurred to him that a man would have to be a damn fool to voluntarily relinquish such a heaven sent family unit!

★   ★   ★

Fully half of the fire starters had perished, but by merging with their comrades the others finally got within easy range. Three blazing arrows arced towards the wagons. By great good fortune two struck the same vehicle, whilst the third extinguished itself deep in the chest of a settler. The man's young wife screamed in horror as he keeled over to lie twitching in his death throes, but everyone else's attention was drawn to the doomed wagon. The tarpaulin ignited with frightening speed and with water unavailable in sufficient quantities, the flames rapidly spread to the sides of the wagon bed. Once they reached the pitch caulking, there would be an unstoppable inferno easily capable of igniting the other wagons.

The settlers looked on with stunned amazement, but William Bent again knew exactly what to do. 'Heave it clear before it's too hot to touch,' he commanded.

Eager men leapt to do his bidding. Far better one wagon burnt out than all of them. The piercing screams that suddenly came from inside took everyone by surprise and then a small, tearstained face appeared. The child appeared dazed and uncertain, as though having awoken from a bad dream.

'Becky!' howled the girl's mother

frantically. Instinctively the woman dashed forward, but William Bent got there quicker. Barging her aside, he clambered up on to the bench seat. Steeling himself against the intense heat, the scout reached inside and grabbed hold of the youngster.

* * *

Deacon Swain possessed an intuitive feel for murder and mayhem. He could sense how things were panning out. Without a leader and having suffered grievous casualties, the Sioux had shot their bolt. He had seen Madden go to ground under the Chandler woman's wagon. It was time for the Kansans to make their move and then clear out while the settlers were still otherwise occupied.

'Fetch the horses, Jim,' he murmured almost imperceptibly. 'And be quick about it. We're about to wear out our welcome with these good people.' So saying, he nodded at the habitually silent third member of his dwindling gang. 'Let's do what we came here to do.' The only response to that was a mirthless grin, but that would suffice.

As Sweet sidled off and Bent retrieved the miraculously unhurt child from the blazing wagon, the two gun thugs slowly and deliberately strode over to the far side of the circle.

Martha spotted them first. As her skin crawled with nervous apprehension, she hissed a warning down to Lee. There was no response, which in itself was disconcerting, but she refrained from snatching a glance. Instead, she raised a Sharps rifle until it was vaguely covering the approaching men.

Revolvers held loosely in their hands, Swain and his mute partner kept on coming until they were about four yards away. Off to their left, there was a fresh outbreak of gunfire as the settlers finally ran off the leaderless and disheartened Sioux war party. Completely ignoring that event, the gunhand instead blatantly scrutinized every inch of Martha

Chandler before remarking conversationally, 'Didn't take you for a man to hide behind a woman's skirt tails, Madden. Then again, they are uncommonly purdy skirt tails.'

Martha flushed with anger. 'A compliment from trash like you is no compliment at all.'

It was Swain's turn to register annoyance. Baring his teeth like a savage beast, he advanced rapidly and brushed her rifle aside as though it were a twig. Whatever he was about to do next was curtailed by Lee's sudden appearance from beneath Rufus Barlow's wagon a short distance away. In his right hand, he held his only remaining Colt Navy, cocked and ready.

After weeks of trying, Swain had finally caught up with his brother's killer. Against such an opponent, retribution would have to be swift. Quickly he glanced off to his right. Sweet was approaching with their horses and his silent partner wore an expression of deadly intent. It was time!

'Get away from that lady, Deacon,' Lee barked. 'Whatever passes between us doesn't concern her.'

'Lady, is it?' Swain queried with a suggestive leer. 'Sounds way too formal to me. But if she's as good as she looks, I would put some cash money down, 'cause I reckon she and I ought to get to know each other better.'

Before Lee could respond to the deliberate provocation, Martha landed a stinging slap across Swain's unshaven face. He'd been hit harder many times before, but the unexpected blow took him completely by surprise and also momentarily distracted his partner. Lee saw his chance and took it. With Martha partially obscuring his mortal enemy, he swivelled slightly to his left and fired at the other grim-faced gunhand. The ball struck that man in the gut, causing him to double over and drop to his knees. The searing pain drew some choice language from his normally sealed lips and reflexively tightened his trigger finger. The revolver discharged harmlessly into the ground as he peered down in stunned disbelief at the blood soaking into his linen shirt.

Fire and move! Lee darted a few paces to his right, so that Martha remained between him and Swain. His bloodied back stung abominably as he dropped on to all fours. He was dimly aware of confused shouting coming from those wagons nearest the most recent Indian attack, but dismissed that from his mind. Another target had already presented itself.

James Sweet was astride his own horse and holding the reins of two more animals behind him. He had been expecting gunplay and so had a revolver to hand, but the outcome was not what he had anticipated. As one man dropped in agony, Sweet attempted to line his weapon up on Madden's solid form, but that man swiftly shifted position and then went to ground. The next thing was a muzzle flash and his horse whinnied with pain and fell back on its haunches. Instinctively throwing himself clear, Sweet landed heavily and knew immediately that he was in big trouble. Shaken up and slightly winded, he was unable to place his opponent. And yet, the next and most likely fatal gunshot just didn't happen.

About to fire again, Lee's peripheral vision warned him that Swain was finally drawing a bead, but because of Martha's close proximity he couldn't risk a shot of his own. Desperately, he threw himself backwards, but only succeeded in whacking his head on a wagon bed. As stars flashed before his eyes, Lee was suddenly in an impossible position and Deacon Swain knew it. With a grunt of satisfaction, that man's finger tightened on the trigger. A set of badly chipped, tobacco-stained teeth were revealed, as a feral grin appeared on his features. This was for his brother!

The Kansas gun thug howled out in agony as Martha's teeth bit savagely into his wrist. His fingers involuntarily expanded and the revolver fell harmlessly out of his grasp. At that moment Swain would have done anything to end the shocking pain and so did the first thing that came to mind. He brought his right knee up into Martha's midriff with savage force. The poor woman emitted a tremendous groan and relaxed her hold on him.

Desperately Lee tried to focus his watery vision. He knew with absolute certainty that Sweet was in front of him and still alive. As it happened, that man was on his knees and aiming directly at Lee's heart. As though by divine intervention there was a powerful crash and James Sweet was thrown backwards to join his dying horse. His forefinger contracted with shock, but the ball merely flew harmlessly off into the endless plains.

Lee had no idea who his saviour was, but he had now twice survived certain death in as many minutes, in addition to miraculously keeping his scalp in his encounter with the Sioux. It was becoming apparent that God was most definitely on his side that day. Even someone as brutalized and ruthless as Deacon Swain recognized that it was time to flee . . . but he fully intended to stack the deck in his favour. Flexing the fingers of his tormented gun hand, he used his other to viciously seize Martha by her long hair.

'You're with me, bitch,' he announced as he dragged her towards the two remaining horses.

A lot of things seemed to happen at once then. Lee recovered all his faculties and leapt to his feet with a levelled revolver. William Bent arrived on the scene with his long gun and Martha's two children erupted in hysterics. Having already lost their father, neither of them could bear to watch their mother being carried off. And yet, it appeared that that was exactly what would happen.

As Lee bellowed out, 'Let her go, or I'll back shoot you,' Swain grabbed a knife from his boot and placed the blade at her throat. Arriving at his horse, he turned and fixed his baleful gaze on Lee. 'This Dutch gal obviously has feelings for you, so unless you want to see her bleed, you'd better holster that pistola, pronto!'

Seething with frustration, Lee slowly lowered his revolver. That wasn't near enough for Swain. 'Lower the hammer and holster it, now!'

Lee reluctantly acquiesced and then called out to all those watching. 'Nobody make any sudden moves. He's not bluffing.'

'Damn right I'm not,' the other man replied as he pulled his captive around to the far side of his animal. He had obviously decided that he stood more chance of getting away if they rode double, because he clambered into the saddle and then pulled her up in front of him. Abandoning the spare horse, he urged his own mount over to the edge of the circle and waited with the blade at Martha's throat while a wagon was wheeled aside. The settlers made no protest. He had already nicked her flesh. Blood trickled down her throat and his deadly intent was there for all to see.

With Fort Laramie in one direction and the remnants of the Sioux war party in another, Swain decided to go back up the steep hill. From such a vantage point he would be able to see off any pursuers and there were still two wagons that had been imperfectly looted. The fact that he had abducted the most attractive woman he'd seen in many a moon was an added bonus. 'Don't even think about slipping off this nag,' he hissed as they moved up towards the plateau. 'I can slice you from ear to ear before you even touch the ground!'

★   ★   ★

Marion tugged insistently at Lee's tattered jacket. 'You can't let him take my ma. You saved me, so save her!'

A totally unexpected voice piped up

behind him. 'I reckon he saved all of us with that crazy charge of his and I for one am grateful.'

Lee turned to find Rufus Barlow with a broad smile on his habitually sour face. That sight alone was so astonishing as to leave him open-mouthed. Then William Bent arrived and only added to it. 'Yeah and it was him shot that other son of a bitch for you. Seems like I didn't break your poking finger after all, eh Rufus?'

That man ruefully raised his heavily-bandaged right hand. 'Oh I think you did. Lucky for me that I was born with two hands.'

After all the fear and violence that had visited them, everyone gave quite a guffaw at that, until Marion very rightly interrupted. 'He's getting away. You've got to do something!'

Lee's back was aching abominably and he was feeling much reduced, but there was no denying she had the right of it. He glanced pointedly over at the powder-stained scout. 'Is that long gun of yours loaded?'

Bent nodded slowly. 'Just what are you thinking?'

'If Swain gets up on to that plateau, we've lost Martha. At best, it'll turn into a man hunt again.' Lee placed a hand on Marion's slight shoulders. 'And we were very lucky with this one.'

'So you want me to drop his horse. That's a mite risky on a hill like that. For the woman, that is.'

Lee felt Marion stiffen under his touch. He wished they could have got the children out of earshot. 'They're halfway up it already, so we don't have much time.'

Bent nodded grimly and moved over to the nearest wagon. For such a shot, he'd need to support the Hawken's long barrel.

Lee looked down at Martha's tearful and apprehensive children. He needed help and they needed occupying. 'Marion, I want you to find my horse and bring him to me. Samuel, I need a bow and a couple of arrows. There's bound to be some out there. Oh, and wrap some material around the arrow-heads and tip some kerosene over them. You'll need to be very careful. Can you do that for me?'

The boy's interest overcame his fear and he nodded eagerly. As the young-sters ran off, Lee joined the scout and began to reload his revolver. He was aware that even though there was plenty that needed doing, all the settlers were watching the drama playing out on the hillside. Swain's animal was struggling with both the heavy load and the incline, but the summit grew ever nearer with every minute that passed.

William Bent retracted the hammer and with great deliberation sighted down the barrel. The distance was not a problem, but he had to take into account the fact that he was firing uphill and that he couldn't allow the large ball to strike either of the riders. It was quite capable of passing right through one of them and on into another.

With the wagon side bearing all the weight, his weapon never wavered as it settled on the horse's hindquarters. In the process of gently inhaling, he suddenly stopped and squeezed the trigger. With a crash that made everyone around him jump, the rifle belched forth its deadly load. Up on the hillside, the horse screamed with pain and collapsed on to the rocky ground. Its riders tumbled clear, alive and apparently unhurt.

Despite the desperate circumstances, the settlers emitted a great cheer and someone called out, 'Hoorah for the mountain man!' As he began to rapidly reload the Hawken, that individual completely ignored the acclaim, because to his mind there was little pleasure to be gained from killing an innocent animal.

As Marion arrived with his horse, Lee gently patted her cheek and stated, 'Well done, Will. I'm going up there after them. If you get a clear shot at that bastard, take it!'

Bent nodded. 'You can count on it. And bring her back in one piece, you hear? Way I see it, you two have got a life together after this.'

Mounting up, Lee looked around for Samuel and smiled broadly when he saw the lad running towards him with a bow and some arrows. Gratefully accepting them, he said, 'Well done, boy,' and then urged his horse over towards the same gap through the wagons that Swain had used. One way or another he would bring Martha back to them . . . alive.

13

As he felt the horse buckle under him, Deacon Swain reacted rapidly. Maintaining a proprietary grip on the woman, he slipped sideways out of the saddle and landed on the hard ground with bruising force. They both avoided breaking any bones, but were now on foot in a harsh and unforgiving land.

'That poxy Hawken,' he snarled. 'I should have killed that goddamned mountain man while I had the chance.' He knew exactly what would happen next and so after staggering to his feet, he kept Martha in front of him, facing the circled wagons. Quickly he snatched the Sharps from the scabbard on his dying horse and began awkwardly backing up the hill, pulling her with him.

Gutsy as ever, she responded, 'He

248

never gave you the chance, you poor oaf!'

The Kansas bushwhacker existed on a short fuse and that comment would surely have ended badly for her, had he not abruptly spotted something that claimed all his attention. Lee Madden had emerged from the defences and was slowly making his way towards the hillside. With a sinking heart, Swain realized that if he tried to shoot it out there and then, he'd leave himself open to the hidden marksman below. His only option was to get up on to the plateau and use the woman as a bargaining chip.

Viciously twisting her hair around his left hand, he hissed, 'Don't push it, bitch. You're only alive because the nights can get cold around these parts.' With that, he nuzzled the nape of her neck and was gratified to feel a tremor pass through her body.

★　★　★

It took many long and nerve-wracking minutes before they finally reached the temporary safety of the plateau. The desperately awkward climb left them both drained and sweating profusely. Glancing wearily around him, Swain took in the two abandoned wagons and decided that the nearest of those would be the place to fort up. His best and only chance for survival was to kill Madden and take his horse. And to do that, the woman would need restraining.

Martha experienced fear and outrage as she found herself roughly tied to the spokes of a wagon wheel. Her eyes briefly locked with his and he sniggered, 'Don't go running off now, you hear?'

She was about to respond, when he again drew his knife. The honed steel caused her to shiver involuntarily, which only caused him more amusement. Moving away, he used the blade to slash through parts of the tarpaulin, so that he could observe the summit.

Cocking his Sharps, he leaned it on the wagon side and settled down to await Madden's arrival.

★   ★   ★

Only a complete buffoon would have gone careering over the brow of the hill and Lee was far from that. Just short of the summit, he dismounted and tethered the reins under a rock. With a Sharps rifle in the crook of his arms, he crawled forward. He knew full well that he and Swain were evenly matched in firearms. It was the Sioux bow slung over his shoulder that might just tip the scales.

Reaching the top, he snatched a quick look, ducked down and then shifted position sideways. The plateau had been deserted except for the two empty wagons. But were they? The tarpaulin on the nearest had been badly torn. Why would the Sioux have bothered to do that?

'He's behind the wagon, Lee!'

Martha had taken a big risk shouting out a warning and she was about to pay for it. With a roar of anger, her captor lashed out . . . hard. If she hadn't been bound to the wagon, the solid backhand slap would have knocked her clean off her feet. With blood trickling from her mashed lips, she only half heard Swain's warning.

'Another word from you, bitch an' juicy or not, I'll open you up for crow bait!'

Lee now knew where they were, but he had no idea of Martha's circumstances. Therefore it seemed to him that his best plan was to first flush the gun thug out. Carefully laying down the cocked rifle, he took out his lucifers and ignited the oily rag that Samuel had tied around one of his arrows. Temporarily leaning the burning projectile against a stone, he then took up his Sharps and quickly fired into the ground next to the wagon. His brief appearance attracted an answering shot, but he had already ducked down and was again on the move to a new position, only this time clutching a bow and arrow.

Drawing the gut bowstring back until the flames were almost licking his fingers, Lee rose up and aimed directly at the wagon bed. The fiery brand flew through the air and slammed into the timber with a solid thwack. In no time at all the bone dry wood was burning. The bow had served its purpose, so Lee abandoned it and raced back for his Sharps. Knowing full well that Swain would have marked his opponent's firing point, he grabbed the gun and continued on to another location. Hunkering down below the crest, he dropped the breechblock and fed in a paper cartridge. As the under lever rose, the block severed the back of the cartridge and so exposed the powder. With a percussion cap in place, he was ready. The question was, what was Deacon Swain up to?

★   ★   ★

Martha's head was still ringing from the vicious blow. It was some time before she appreciated the frightening turn of events. She was tethered to a burning wagon and her captor appeared to have just made up his mind about something.

'If Madden wants you alive, he's going to have to break cover.' With that, he moved to the edge of the wagon. On the far side of it, flames were licking the tarpaulin. It wouldn't be long before the whole vehicle was ablaze, so he couldn't stay there. It was in his mind to make a dash for the rocks where he had originally lain in wait. From there he could maybe pick Lee Madden off and then take his horse.

'You hear me, Madden? I've tied this little lady to the wagon. Unless you want her lookin' like a turkey roast, you'd better come running!'

Turning to face Martha, he favoured her with a sick smirk. 'Huh, you'd better hope he likes you. If not, I'll maybe see you in hell, bitch!' Swinging his rifle around the side, he fired for effect and then threw himself out into the open. Before the report of that shot had even died away, he was already halfway to the rocks.

Martha couldn't help herself. As the scorching heat swept over her she screamed out, 'For Christ's sake, Lee, I'm going to burn to death! Don't leave me!'

Even though aware of Swain hightailing it for the hills, Lee had no choice and he knew it. Come what may, he had to rescue Martha Chandler. Jumping to his feet, he bellowed down to the circled wagons, 'Will, I need you up here with that long gun, pronto!'

Without awaiting a response, he sprinted for the blazing wagon. In truth he was sick with worry. The thought that he had started the fire that might kill her was just too much to bear.

Down below, William Bent mounted up and headed out of the circle. 'You folks reload anything and everything. I don't figure that those heathens'll be back, but you never can tell.' With that, he happily left them to it. He was mighty sick of nurse-maiding them anyway, especially as there seemed to be no end to it. Hell, they hadn't even crossed the Rockies yet!

If he hadn't been so intent on getting up to the plateau with all speed, he might have noticed young Thad Wells following on behind on foot. In his hand was a deadly Colt Navy, purloined from one of the settlers!

★   ★   ★

'Oh, thank God!' Martha exclaimed as Lee burst into view. She had been frantically tugging against her bonds and her wrists were smeared with blood. With all the tarpaulin now alight, she was at full stretch and shielding her face from the inferno. The smell of her own burning hair had reached her nostrils and raw terror had taken hold.

Endeavouring to keep the wagon between him and the rocks, Lee sliced into the rope with his knife. Suddenly free, Martha tumbled to the ground just as a gunshot rang out. The ball slammed into the burning timber, mere inches from his face. Dropping to the ground, Martha's rescuer rolled over to her. Unceremoniously grabbing her around the waist, he half-carried, half-dragged the dazed woman back behind the wagon, so that they were both shielded from Swain's shooting.

Drawing in a deep breath, Lee bellowed, 'Are you out there, Will?'

'You'd better believe it,' came the reassuring response.

Despite the ever-present pain in his back, Lee felt a surge of savage joy. 'So let's finish this,' he hollered back, before turning to Martha. Gently stroking her hair, he said, 'You stay here and keep out of sight. This won't take long.'

She gazed up at him as though only just coming to terms with her survival. 'You came for me!'

He chuckled. 'You told me not to disappear again, remember?' With that, he was up and running, off at an angle so as to confuse Swain.

*   *   *

The moment he heard William Bent's voice, Deacon Swain began to feel like an item of hunted prey. The knowledge that there was now a big Hawken rifle up on the plateau was distinctly unnerving. Then Madden dashed into view and he instinctively tried for a shot. There was a crash over by the crest and he felt the blast of pressure as a large ball flew past his head. As a result, although his own Sharps discharged, his shot went hopelessly wide.

'Your time is up, scum belly,' came the scout's mocking call and Swain was actually lost for words. Beads of sweat coated his forehead as he dropped into a crouch and began to retreat into the rocks. He knew full well that with the two of them working together, Bent could keep him pinned down whilst Madden moved in for the kill. It was exactly what he would have done.

Desperately twisting around, searching for any avenue of escape, he suddenly froze with shock. There was someone or something behind him! But how could that be? With a snarl of rage, he rose to his full height and whirled about, firing as soon as his gun muzzle settled on the target. The rifle ball struck the man just right of centre and would have likely proved fatal . . . had he not already been dead!

With abject horror, Swain stared into Brady's sightless eyes. His appearance was the stuff nightmares are made from. Most of the man's hair was missing and his features were frozen into a horrified mask, coated with dried blood. A great slit in his throat gave every impression of being another orifice. The ghastly corpse lay propped against a large boulder, its final resting place after having been casually hurled from the cliff above.

Brutalized as he was to all aspects of violence, it still took a moment or so for

Swain to recover his wits and by then it was far too late. Again the Hawken crashed out and this time Bent didn't miss. The .50 calibre ball struck Swain in the upper back and sent him tumbling forward into the arms of his former accomplice.

★   ★   ★

Seeing his mortal enemy fall, Lee threw caution to the wind and raced forward. Without bothering to zigzag, he was in amongst the rocks in seconds. Knowing exactly where his enemy was, he had the butt of his Sharps tucked tightly into his shoulder, left eye closed, right eye peering straight down the barrel. And then, without any difficulty, he found him.

Finally coming face to face with Deacon Swain was something of a shock. Lee had expected to just shoot him out of hand, but finding that man badly wounded, lying next to his mutilated crony, completely took the wind out of his sails. He just stood there, forefinger curled around the trigger, as though in a trance. Swain was too badly hurt to even provide his customary sneer. Then the memories came flooding back. A red mist seemed to form before his eyes and he began to squeeze.

'You killed my brother,' he murmured with deadly intent.

'And you killed mine, you cockchafer!'

'He needed killing. Which was more than my wife did!'

'That was just an accident and you know it!' Swain retorted as he winced with pain.

'Maybe, maybe not,' Lee grudgingly allowed. 'But killing Jake wasn't!'

The two men stared at each other, linked by mutual loathing, but still Lee couldn't quite bring himself to end it.

'My my, this *is* cosy!' William Bent had arrived and was observing the strange stand-off. 'Those two don't look so good,' he remarked drily.

And quite abruptly all the tension drained out of Lee and he allowed the Sharps to tilt forward. He suddenly felt so desperately tired. What had all that hatred and violence back in Kansas achieved?

'So are you gonna shoot him or what?' Bent persisted.

As Lee replied, his eyes never left those of his nemesis. 'I've had a belly full of killing. I'm going to take him back to Fort Laramie to face justice. If he survives the journey, his fate will be in the army's hands, not mine.'

Bent snorted like a horse. 'That's just plum crazy. Even if you do make it, you'll likely be arrested as well.'

'I'll take my chances,' Lee responded with bitter resolve.

'And what about that Chandler woman? Does she really deserve yet more grief?'

The gunshot took everyone by surprise. The right side of Deacon Swain's head exploded like a ripe melon. His body jerked under the impact, before slumping to one side. He was quite dead!

Both men whirled around, guns at the ready. Before them stood the tearful, but very determined figure of Thad Wells. As the smoking revolver slipped from his hand, he stated very simply, 'That man killed my pa!'

14

The little group of four slowly descended the steep hill. With the exception of the mountain man, they were all lost in their own thoughts. So it was that he alone spotted the distant column of horsemen as it approached the circled wagons. The hairs went up on the back of his neck as he mumbled, 'Sweet Jesus, not again!'

His companions all looked up in alarm. As Martha's gaze took in the newcomers, she instinctively clung to Lee Madden. 'Surely those savages won't try again,' she cried out in horror.

Under any other circumstances that man would have welcomed the contact, but as it was his back spasmed from the pain of her sudden pressure. Wincing, he stared long and hard at the advancing riders. He wasn't too sure what a formation of Indians on the move looked like, but after his service in the Mexican War he could certainly distinguish an army column.

'Those ain't Sioux or any other painted heathens. Them's blue bellies, by God!'

Bent shook his head in disbelief. 'Which means that they're still looking for you. You must have *really* annoyed that lieutenant back in Fort Laramie.'

Martha seemed to get a new lease of life. Speeding up her descent, she announced, 'We've got to get down there fast and get you under cover, Lee.'

'What if they want to search the wagons this time?' queried Bent with unhelpful pessimism.

'Well then we won't let them,' she replied stubbornly.

The makings of a smile surfaced on Bent's craggy features, but he held his peace and concentrated instead on not breaking his neck.

It seemed an age before the tired and dusty soldiers finally fetched up before the wagons. There were twenty-two non-coms and enlisted men led by a young second lieutenant. Although quite obviously stunned at the highly visible carnage, he was trying his level best to appear experienced in front of his men. 'Looks like you folks have had quite a shindig. It's a good job we happened by.'

That was just too much for Rufus Barlow, who seemed to have grown in stature as a result of the Indian attack. 'Why?' he demanded brusquely. 'We drove those savages off without any help from the army. I thought you soldier boys were out here to protect us, but you've done damn all!'

Before the chastened young officer had time to protest, William Bent got down to what was on everybody's mind. 'Just what brings you out here, Lieutenant? Don't tell me you're still

266

chasing shadows?'

It was a grizzled sergeant that answered that. 'It weren't no shadow that locked Lieutenant Fleming in his own guardhouse, mister and he ain't of a mind to let it drop.'

His officer finally got his second wind. 'My name is Lieutenant Reno and I've got orders to search these wagons for the fugitive, Madden. My superior, Mr Fleming won't take no for an answer. Not that we don't trust you, mind,' he quickly added with one eye on Rufus.

There was an uncomfortable silence as the settlers digested the implications of that demand. They all knew exactly where Lee was; not ten yards from the army detail's commander and now that Swain was dead, he didn't intend to go into captivity peacefully. It was lucky for everyone that Bent was one step ahead.

'I can save you and your men a whole lot of trouble, Lieutenant. Lee Madden's dead as a wagon tyre, but I'll tell you this. If it hadn't been for him, I doubt that we could have held those varmints off.'

The young man was momentarily flummoxed, but not so the sergeant. 'So where's the body? Injuns aren't known for carrying dead white men off.'

Cool as anything, the scout replied, 'Up on the plateau. Off in the rocks a ways. He was cut up some, mind. He and another fellow made a stand against a band of Sioux.'

That finally gave the lieutenant something solid to work on. 'Sergeant, you and Cooke get on up there. If it is him, we can finally report back to the fort.'

As the two men reluctantly departed for the steep climb, Reno offered by way of explanation, 'Private Cooke was in the guardhouse with Lieutenant Fleming. He's the only one of my men that can recognize the fugitive, so one way or another we'll settle this matter.'

Martha glanced anxiously at Bent,

but that man just smiled knowingly and went about his business.

★   ★   ★

It was quite some time before the two soldiers returned. The sergeant appeared to be unaffected by their gruesome reconnaissance, but there was no disguising Cooke's discomfort. Despite the heat, his face was pale and there were traces of spittle around his mouth. Not that his officer showed any sympathy. Having kicked his heels amongst the unwelcoming settlers for far too long, Reno was keen to be off.

'Well, was it him, Private?'

The enlisted man merely blurted out unhelpfully, 'Jesus, what a mess, sir!'

'If you say so, but was it him?' Reno demanded impatiently.

Private Cooke shrugged. 'I guess so, sir. You couldn't hardly tell after what those Injuns had done to him.'

'So you're sure then?' persisted Reno pointedly.

Cooke plainly didn't relish the limelight and was keen to rejoin the other enlisted men. 'Yes sir, it was Madden.'

Lieutenant Reno slapped his gauntlets together with satisfaction. 'Well that settles it.'

'Won't Mr Fleming want to see the body, sir?' queried the non-com.

The young officer had had more than enough. 'He'll see my report. That'll have to suffice. Now move them out, Sergeant.'

With a keen eye for the ladies, Reno tipped his hat to Martha. 'We'll be leaving you now, miss. If we rub up against any of those hostiles, we'll be sure to give them a bloody nose for you.'

Bent groaned and theatrically spat in the earth, whilst Rufus offered a sarcastic retort. 'Oh, well hurrah for the US Army!'

Colouring brightly, the embarrassed young man rejoined his men. As the bluecoats set off, the sergeant could be heard saying, 'There was another fella up there with Madden, sir.'

'I know,' replied Reno with obvious disinterest. 'If you remember, that white haired civilian said as much.'

'Shot all to hell,' persisted the non-com. 'I'm sure I've seen him someplace before.'

Reno had heard enough from everybody. 'Leave it be, Sergeant. Unless you want to lose one of those stripes.'

And with that, they were gone.

★ ★ ★

It wasn't until the army detail was a mere speck on the horizon that Martha allowed a jaded Lee Madden out of the wagon bed. She could tell by the way he moved that his back was troubling him.

'That wound's going to need some stitches,' she stated, gently but firmly. 'And I'm the person to do it.'

Lee glanced over at William Bent and that man winked broadly. 'Fair enough,' he accepted. 'Only keep that damned whiskey well away from it, huh?' Then, on a crazy impulse, he suddenly took Martha in his arms and kissed her full on the lips. Surprise, then pleasure registered on her lovely features.

'You know something?' she murmured. 'I think we're going to make it to Oregon after all.'

'Damn right we are!'

NOTHING MORE TO LOSE

Tyler Hatch

The day Buck Buckley foils the Green River bank robbery is the day he becomes a hero with a capital 'H' — although the attention that follows is the last thing he wants or needs. Locals can't understand Buckley's resistance, but they do not know the secrets he is hiding. When his picture appears in the papers, his past begins to catch up with him. And as his newfound fame puts him in the firing line, he must stop running and address his demons face on in a final showdown.